A LISA DAVIS MYSTERY
THE THIRD VICTIM

Lilla M. Waltch

Dodd, Mead & Company   New York

For Mark,
Amy, Alison, and Bonnie
With love

Published by Dodd, Mead & Company, Inc.
71 Fifth Avenue, New York, NY 10011
Distributed in Canada by
McClelland and Stewart Ltd., Toronto
Manufactured in the United States of America
First Edition

1   2   3   4   5   6   7   8   9   10

Library of Congress Cataloging-in-Publication Data

Waltch, Lilla M.
    The third victim.

    I. Title.
PS3573.A47227t4   1987   813'.54   86-32834
ISBN 0-396-08942-9

ISBN 0-396-08942-9

CHAPTER 1

Tuesday Morning, April 24, 1984

Lisa stopped at Silverman's office door and read the typed note under his nameplate. PLEASE DO NOT DISTURB. She checked her watch. 10:05. Usually he came out to the lounge and called her in when he was ready to see her. Maybe he'd meant to cancel their appointment today. He'd done so before, but never without notice. She felt a stab of annoyance. Some of what she'd often heard Madeline say about the man was true. He was condescending toward women and he was always on the make.

She remembered that time in his office when he put his hand on her arm and stroked it gently as he said, "I can teach you a great deal. You have the kind of mind I would love to touch." Lisa felt her lips twitching into a smile even now as she remembered how ridiculous he'd seemed. His voice had been low and sort of whispery. His nearly black eyes had grown moist with phony sincerity. At his touch, she'd jumped out of her chair as if she had sat on a pin and said, almost calmly, "I don't want anyone to touch my mind. Not anyone. I do my own learning, in my own way."

1

He'd retreated immediately. "Whoa, girl. It's just my way of saying that you're going to do fine as a T.A. in my course."

"Okay, okay," she said, walking backward while looking him in the eye, like a lion tamer pretending to dominate an unreliable beast.

Back in the English Department lounge Lisa heard the bells of the campus chapel strike the quarter hour, one short peal. The two other occupants of the lounge, who had been reading with concentration, stirred. Bob Applewhite lifted his monklike face as if to receive a blessing and then bowed his head so that only his bald dome with its fringe of hair was visible. Madeline Jennings-Ellison, a small-boned blonde, looked up with a frown as if waking from a bad dream.

Madeline closed her book and riffled through her papers until she found what she was looking for, a copy of yesterday's *Addison News*. "Did you see this?" she asked, thrusting a newspaper at Lisa. Her voice, low and grating, was a surprising contrast to her delicate prettiness.

Lisa leaned forward and saw the photograph Madeline was tapping with her finger, a dark-haired, bearded man in his late thirties with glasses and a wide smile. SILVERMAN APPOINTED TO FINSTERMANN CHAIR, she read. "Yes, I saw it," Lisa said softly, aware that Bob Applewhite was trying to study in his corner.

Madeline thumped the photograph. "That asshole."

Bob Applewhite looked up, startled either by her language or by the angry growl of her voice.

Lisa began to pick up her papers and cram them into her briefcase. Madeline was a feminist with a chip on her shoulder the size of a pine log, and Professor Sheldon Silverman was one of her pet peeves. Lisa was tired of listening to her.

"That asshole," Madeline repeated more forcefully. "He doesn't deserve it."

"I imagine he got it for his teaching and his new book, not his behavior," Lisa said. Silverman's womanizing was legendary in the department. There was even a rumor that Madeline had been taken in by him at one time, although Lisa didn't know whether it was true.

Bob Applewhite looked up and began to protest, "Could you please . . ." in his frightened voice.

"I'm just leaving," Lisa said.

In the doorway she nearly bumped into Mary Reardon, who was carrying her empty coffee mug. The big, red-haired woman patted Lisa's arm. "I've been looking for you. Where you off to?"

"My weekly think tank with Silverman."

"Ah, the beast in his lair," Mary said, tossing her head in the direction of Silverman's office. She was a visiting professor at Addison this year and claimed she had never run into a faculty member anywhere who behaved as badly as Silverman. "Lunch today?" she asked Lisa.

"Slop or food?"

"I'm afraid it'll have to be slop," Mary replied. "I've students coming in right after."

"Okay. See you in the cafeteria, then."

In the English Department office Edith Waks sat bent forward, elbows on her desk, fists in her cheeks, reading a Xeroxed sheet. She looked up as Lisa approached. In her fifties, widowed, Edith made the English Department her life. Every morning she dressed in soft pastel blouses with billowy sleeves and dainty high-heeled pumps as if she were going to sell perfume at Bloomingdale's. Her hair was frosted blonde, her eyelids stained purple or royal blue. Her sparkling necklaces and earrings echoed the hope in her dark brown eyes. She was looking for a life. A man would be best, but if not a man, at least she wanted to be part of other people's lives. At Addison she made sure that she was.

"I've an appointment with Silverman," Lisa said, trying not to breathe the heavy waves of Tabu that undulated around Edith, "but he doesn't answer and there's a do-not-disturb note on his door."

"It was there this morning when I arrived," Edith said. "Guess he came in early to work, but I haven't seen him yet. Why don't you just go in. I'll take responsibility if he's a bear. Here, give him these." She thrust a pile of mail and notices at Lisa.

In front of Silverman's door, Lisa knocked. Then she opened the door gently and peered in around the edge.

The impact of what she saw threw her against the door frame. For a few moments she simply stared, unable to move or speak. There was blood everywhere—smeared on the walls, on the desk top, on the papers and books strewn about the room as if caught up in a tornado. Blood congealed in puddles on Silverman's desk chair. And there, on the floor face up in the midst of this devastation, eyes open as if staring at the ceiling, lay Sheldon Silverman, Professor of American Literature and Journalism, one arm flung over his head, the other clutching his heart as if he'd had a sudden pain. He was covered with blood—his face, chest, arms, and legs, his clothes stiff with it. Lisa wrenched her eyes away from his body.

His coffee mug lay shattered on the floor beside him, the dark brown of spilled coffee mingled with the deep-hued reddish brown blood pooled on the parquet floor. Lisa had watched him sip black coffee from that mug, a sixties me-

mento, when she met with him to discuss her teaching assignments. A large fragment of cream-colored china rested near the door, almost near enough to touch with her toe. On it were the blue-painted dove and the bright blue letters: P, E, A . . . The missing final letters, "C, E," whispered in Lisa's head and, suddenly, without even knowing she was doing so, she began to scream. The papers she'd been carrying fluttered to the floor. She barely heard the shouts and the clatter of feet as people came running from the lounge, the English Department office, and nearby offices.

CHAPTER 2

Tuesday, April 23, 1968

It is springtime. Late sixties. On the grassy slopes of a hilly upstate New York college campus, students are spread out in clusters, sunbathing, enjoying the bright sunshine and brilliant blue sky of a magnificent day.

The three young men trudging up the steep wooded hill behind the campus look very much like the carefree students gathered on the green slopes in front of the concrete-and-glass building that dominates the hill. They, too, are wearing the uniform of the times: blue workshirts, jeans, ankle-high orange workboots. Their hair is long. The youngest of the three, Danny Connors, is big and muscular. His taffy-colored hair is tied securely back in a long thick pony tail, but it frizzes around his face in a halo of golden curls. "Maybe we should have made this inspection trip at night when there's little chance of meeting up with anyone, Shel," he says.

The young man to whom he speaks is of medium height. His face is lean and sharp-featured with shaggy black eyebrows, dark wavy hair to his shoulders, and a luxuriant beard as glossy as sealskin. Sunlight turns his glasses into circles of gold. "No," he replies with authority. "We have to pick out a place to meet after the job is done and plan alternate routes of escape in case anything goes wrong. Can't see well enough at night. Don't worry. No one ever goes back here."

The third man, much taller than the other two and so lean that he seems emaciated, looks around anxiously at the dense undergrowth and the thickly growing trees that are just beginning to leaf. "I hope you're right," he mutters. "All we need is to have anyone see Danny and me with you. Then when it happens, they'll pin it on the three of us for sure."

Shel makes a contemptuous sound in his throat. "Oh, don't be so paranoid, Jim," he says. "As far as anyone at Page University knows, we hardly know each other—just belong to some of the same political groups, is all."

Jim grunts and gives Shel a look as if to say, What the hell do you know about anything?

"You've got no worries. I'm the one they'll be looking at," Shel says proudly, "not you. I'm the one with the SDS connection." He feels a wave of revulsion toward Jim, who has been a pain in the ass right from the start with his doubts and complaints. He questions everything Shel says, yet he doesn't have the balls to do anything on his own. And Shel hates the way Danny looks up to Jim and follows him around like a younger brother. I'm the one with the guts and ideas, Shel thinks. I deserve better than these two. But there are no others he could trust to help. Although there are many so-called radicals on campus, so far no one has done anything more than march around carrying signs and chanting slogans. No one has burned his draft card. Or taken over a building, like they've been doing at Columbia. Shel believes it is time to change the tempo of protest, to show the military-industrial establishment that there are some radicals who are not content to stand around chanting. Throughout the country incidents are beginning to occur. Draft card burnings. Fires set in induction centers. Blood poured over draft files. Even bombings. Shel believes there is a gathering flood of purpose behind the passive marchers if only it can be tapped by individuals brave enough to take chances. Individuals like himself. Jim and Danny are the only others he knows who feel as he does. He needs them.

Shel climbs the hill toward the rear of the large concrete building. The others follow.

"There's only one thing that worries me," Danny says in his gentle way. "The experiment I've been working on. Sam's baby."

"Sam Harrison?" Shel asks.

Danny nods. "He's been breeding these rats with sensitized immune genes through hundreds of generations. He's just about got the proof he needs to back up a whole new theory of immunology. He has his eye on a Nobel Prize."

Jim whistles. "A Nobel. You're kidding. It's that good?"

"Every bit," Danny assures him. "It may be the first step toward a cure for cancer." Danny shakes his bright head sadly. "He's not received recognition. He's counting on this, surely."

"Why are you so sure his rats will be harmed?" Shel asks.

"I'm not sure about anything. But those rats are in the next lab. He takes care of them like blessed babies. I'd not want him looking to me if they're blown sky-high."

Shel waves a hand as if to dismiss the argument. "I know Sam Harrison. He's as opposed to this war as any of the rest of us. He may not like losing his rats, but he'll understand."

Danny gives a short laugh. "I wouldn't be too sure of that."

"But the real point," Shel intones, "is that whether Sam Harrison likes it or not, we're fighting for a cause that is more important than his rats. More important than any individual or any group. We're fighting for all humanity. We're fighting to free human beings from their chains."

Jim snorts and says, "Hey, Shel, I'm worried about you. Delusions of grandeur and all that. You're beginning to sound like Karl Marx."

Shel ignores him and continues in rising ministerial tones, "I believe in the perfectibility of mankind. I believe we can overcome the limitations of society, transcend the military-industrial state. That we can be free!" He stands directly in front of Jim, challenging him, but feels as if he is floating above him, like Gabriel delivering the Word. Just last night Shel used these same words about the perfectibility of mankind to Cindy Stevens, one of his freshman writing tutees. They were sitting on a hooked rug in front of the fireplace in his rented cottage, looking over her last paper.

She breathed in sharply at the impact of his words, her brown bangs, burnished red by the firelight, falling into her eyes.

"Free," he said. "We can be free." And her firm knees had parted, her muscular swimmer's thighs had held his head tightly between her legs in a drowning person's grip as he tasted her secret brine.

Facing Jim, Shel smiles to himself, like Ali Baba who has discovered the magic words, "Open Sesame." With his words he unlocks the caves where treasures lay.

"You're carried away with your own rhetoric," Jim says disgustedly.

"If you don't believe in the principles behind what you're

doing, you better get your ass back into the lab," Shel says. What a jerk this guy is. In it up to his ears, and he has no idea of the scope of the operation. Shel thinks of Jim's pale wife, her limp, almost-white hair framing a serious round face. A peacenik herself, known on campus as one of those slightly crazy, dedicated types. He hopes Jim has kept his pledge of secrecy.

Jim turns away, sullen. Words are not his forte. And Danny breaks in, still worrying about Sam Harrison. "You don't know him the way I do. Ever since his bitch of a wife walked out on him, it's his work that he lives for, and that's a fact."

"Well, that's tough," Shel says low and angry. "We must all be ready to sacrifice for the Movement. Even our lives."

Danny nods. He's told them often that in his country to lay down your life for freedom is considered an honor. He's a Derry lad. He's never known peace. He was born into the Troubles.

Reluctantly, Jim nods as well, accepting Shel's fervor.

Shel climbs up the steepest part of the hill, strides toward a thicket of low evergreens. "In case of any trouble, this is where we'll meet and plan our strategy."

The three men look up at the rear of Lohr Science Center through the trees. Danny Connors points out the location of the lab on the third floor where a secret Defense Department contract to develop an incendiary substance one hundred times more lethal than napalm is being worked on by a team of Page University chemists. They look solemnly at the corner of the building and then back at one another, their faces glowing with purpose.

Shel grasps their arms and says, "As Che said, 'The true revolutionary is guided by strong feelings of love.' " Looking up at the bright blue sky veined with a myriad of tree branches, he sees a vision of Cindy Stevens's perfect young flesh. He can use the Che Guevara quote with her tonight. She has told him that her life lacks purpose, that something is missing. She has told him how much she admires his sense of conviction. Shel can't wait to be with her again, to fill her with his purpose.

CHAPTER 3

Later Tuesday Morning, April 24, 1984

Lieutenant Irving Cohen eased himself into the large vinyl armchair that dominated the English Department lounge. In his late forties, he wore a shapeless gray suit and some extra pounds that made him look older. He held a handkerchief to weepy red eyes. Officer Hughes, Cohen's assistant, sat beside his superior and watched his every move like a dog trained to anticipate his master's commands. Hughes was good-looking despite the too-bright brown checked jacket and brown slacks, Lisa thought as she took another sip from the Styrofoam cup of water that Edith Waks had given her right after she'd found Professor Silverman's body.

Cohen was looking around the room, assessing its occupants, when suddenly his body began to twitch violently. "It's the . . . ah . . ." He stopped a sneeze by closing his eyes and mouth and wrinkling up his large nose until the sneeze was trapped forcibly inside his huge body. Lisa felt her nose beginning to twitch sympathetically for him. ". . . pollen!" he finished explosively. He'd be better off if he just sneezed, Lisa thought.

Wiping his face energetically with his large white handkerchief, the lieutenant looked around the room keenly as if trying to pick out the murderer. Suddenly he got up and strode over to a vase of forsythia on the refectory table in the corner. "Do you mind?" he asked the room in general.

"No," and "Of course not," everyone murmured.

Holding it away from him as if it were a live firecracker, Cohen opened the door of the lounge and deposited the vase in the hall. He returned to his chair, looked around the room again, searching each face as he continued to sniff and rub his nose vigorously. Just as he was about to speak, another powerful spasm shook his body, and this time he did sneeze. His body seemed to explode, to shake from the top of his head right down to his toes as he let go into his waiting handkerchief.

As soon as he could speak, he turned to his assistant. "Hughes, get the windows," he commanded.

The younger man got up obediently and closed the three leaded casement windows through which gentle breezes had been blowing. Within moments the room was oppressively warm.

Cohen scanned the faces in the room. Everyone seemed to squirm uncomfortably as if he had something to hide. The heat covered them like a blanket. Lisa couldn't get the image of Silverman lying in all that blood out of her mind. She knew he had been shot many times, but it was the memory of his eyes, wide open, staring at the ceiling, that troubled her the most. Why did his eyes bother her so much? she wondered. It was because his open eyes made him look so alive, she thought. That's why they close dead people's eyes, so they'll look dead, so you'll really believe they're dead. She shuddered and closed her own eyes tightly. When she opened them, Lieutenant Cohen was looking at her speculatively.

"This won't take long," he said. "Just some general information and then I'll make individual appointments for you to come into the station. By then we'll have some results from the postmortem on Professor Silverman and we'll have a better idea when the crime occurred. Meanwhile, you can all work on your alibis." He said it with a straight face, and they all nodded, although they looked a bit puzzled. Only Officer Hughes laughed. He had a nice laugh. At least his laugh was his own, not tailored to please his superior, Lisa thought.

Professor Froming was fidgeting, crossing and recrossing thin legs covered in gray flannel. He didn't seem comfortable sitting on the sofa between Madeline Jennings-Ellison and Mary Reardon. A small wary man, he seemed even smaller now, wedged in as he was between Madeline, who was compact yet curvaceous, and the ample Mary, whose large pillowy bosom and rounded hips fit snugly into her usual tweed suit. Lisa couldn't help but smile at the look of discomfort on Froming's small, pinched face.

Mary caught Lisa's eye and winked as if she knew exactly what Lisa was smiling about. It was just this kind of understanding between them that had led to their becoming good friends, despite the difference in their positions, since they had both come to Addison in early September. Turning back to face the police detectives, Lisa wondered if it was only her imagination that Lieutenant Cohen seemed to catch the look that passed between Mary and her and file it away for future reference.

"We'll just go around the room," the lieutenant was saying, "and you can give me your names and your positions here at the university . . ." His manner was pleasant, almost jocular, but Lisa perceived a toughness beneath it. He turned toward Professor Louis Hammer, who sat on the other side of Hughes, and nodded his head. "Would you please begin."

Professor Hammer leaned forward in his chair, lank brown hair falling into his eyes. His face was asymmetrical, with large features—a sharp nose and strong cheekbones tapering down to a weak chin and prominent Adam's apple that was now working up and down in the grip of some powerful emotion, like a ball on a string. Lisa thought she had never seen anyone look so nervous.

"Please excuse me, Lieutenant, uh . . ."

"Cohen," Cohen supplied crisply.

"Uh, yes, Lieutenant Cohen. Shel Silverman was one of my oldest friends. I'm not used to the idea that he's . . . ah . . . dead. And so brutally. Murdered . . . I . . ."

"Yes, of course." Cohen cut in without sympathy. "Your name. Your position. And relationship to the deceased."

Lieutenant Cohen's businesslike tone seemed to calm Hammer. He spoke up in a clear voice, "Assistant Professor Louis Jason Hammer. Professor of American Literature. I'm an old friend and colleague of Professor Silverman."

Next was Bob Applewhite, crouched on a hassock at Hammer's feet. As Bob told them that he was a graduate student working in the field of metaphysical poetry with Professor Froming and made his appointment for an interview with the police, Lisa continued to study Hammer. He was a graceless man, somehow misshapen, yet she was not sure exactly how. She sat in on his course in American poetry. But not for long. The man was a fool. Everything he said was memorized from books. Listening to him talk, she'd doubted whether he'd ever had a thought of his own. After a few classes, she'd stopped going. Yet, strangely enough, he had published a fine book on Wallace Stevens as well as some interesting articles on other modern poets in *American Literary Studies,* one of the best literary journals.

Edith Waks entered the lounge and closed the door softly behind her. Lieutenant Cohen was busy with his handkerchief again, but he looked up at her expectantly. She said, "I've sent messengers to the classrooms to cancel English classes for this period. We won't be disturbed." Her face was blotched, her eyes swollen and as red as the lieutenant's.

"Thank you," he said. He blew his nose again. Lisa held her wet jersey away from her skin. Her jeans were sticking to her. The third degree with closed windows instead of bright lights, she thought.

Edith perched on the arm of the sofa next to Mary as Lieutenant Cohen began to interview the three people sitting there. First Mary, then Froming, and finally Madeline were made short work of; their identities established, times for interviews arranged, and it was Lisa's turn.

"Lisa Davis. Graduate student. T.A. in Professor Silverman's course in American Journalism."

"T.A.?" Cohen questioned.

"Teaching Assistant. I sit in on the course and I teach a section, a small group."

As she spoke, Officer Hughes scribbled in his notebook.

"Relationship to deceased?"

"None beyond my serving as T.A. for his course. I met with him weekly."

"And you found the body?"

"Yes. I had a ten o'clock appointment with him this morning. I knocked on his office door. He'd . . . somebody had . . . put up a do-not-disturb note. I knocked. When he didn't answer, I opened the door. I saw him." She stopped talking. She was trembling as if she were holding on to a live wire.

Edith Waks was the last to be interviewed. After her appointment was set up, the lieutenant said, "Thank you, Mrs. Waks. I'll stop by the office for your complete list of English faculty and graduate students, Professor Silverman's student lists, and the names of any other people who might have come in to see him in the last few weeks."

Lisa watched the trim secretary as she nodded cooperatively, her head to one side like an attentive bird's. Today Edith was wearing something soft and lavender with some kind of sparkly brooch at her throat. If anything, she seemed calmer and more efficient than usual. Only her red face and swollen eyes betrayed emotion. Lisa tried to imagine the stylish widow in the midst of a torrid affair with Silverman. Dumped by him. Then stalking him with a revolver, shooting him, and attaching a do-not-disturb sign to his office door with Scotch tape before going back to her Xerox machine in the English office. She couldn't imagine it. And she couldn't imagine any of the people sitting around the room murdering Silverman either. English professors were a quiet lot, introspective, worrying about things like student evaluations and grants and tenure. Murder? Lisa shook her head, surveying the group.

Lieutenant Cohen sat back in his chair. "As you'll see when you leave, Professor Silverman's office is being examined by my criminal investigation team. When they're finished, his office will be sealed off pending further notice. Please stop by the English Department on your way out. The fingerprint men are set up there. I want prints from everyone." He got to his feet, sniffing. "See you tomorrow." Hughes followed him out.

After the detectives had left the room, the group seated

around the lounge sat silently for a few moments as if in shock. Edith Waks was the first to move. "I better go and get him that information," she said as she left.

The rest of them reacted with appropriate dismay at the brutal murder of a colleague and friend, if he had been a friend to any of them.

As Lisa passed Silverman's office, the door opened and a man carrying a large black case stepped out, closing the door behind him. Lisa caught a glimpse of a man with a camera, a blinding flash of light. Several other men were working around the room. In the English office, she joined a line waiting to have their fingers inked. Mary was being fingerprinted by a blue-uniformed policewoman. She waved inky fingers in Lisa's direction. In front of Lisa, Professor Froming and Bob Applewhite were deep in conversation about some poet whose name sounded like Swindle.

Sam Harrison appeared in the doorway. He stopped stock-still taking in the unusual scene before him. Then he hurried to Lisa's side. "What's going on, a mass arrest for murdering the English language?" He kissed her on the cheek despite the people all around them.

"Oh, Sam," she sighed, accepting his kiss and the comfort of his solid presence. "This is no joking matter. There's been a murder, all right. Silverman. I found him."

Sam put his arm around her. As always, his very presence made her feel safe. Safe and loved. It wasn't just that he was so much older than she was. It was the kind of person he was. Considerate. Caring. Dependable. Everything that Brad Newman, her former boyfriend, was not. Sam waited with her until it was her turn, even though it meant being late for the graduate seminar in biochemistry research methods he taught.

CHAPTER 4

Monday, April 29, 1968

Shel is waiting for them in the basement of his rented cottage on this moist April night, fragrant with the beginning blossoms of spring. He sees their shadows passing across the frosted basement window, high up near the ceiling, and he is standing by the basement door when their soft knocking begins. Their faces reflect his own excitement. They clasp one another's hands.

"Welcome, brothers," Shel says, his voice trembling.

Jim and Danny hurry inside. Danny carries a heavy briefcase that he puts down in a corner of the concrete floor next to a wooden crate covered with a khaki-colored poncho.

"How're my babies?" Jim asks tenderly, lifting the corner of the poncho. He is responsible for acquiring the sticks of dynamite on which their plan depends. During the summer in his part-time job as a laborer for a construction company, he managed to slip them out, undetected, one by one. He brought the sticks to Shel's basement individually and packed them carefully into the wooden crate.

Shel feels annoyed at the proprietary tone in Jim's voice. He has lectured both Jim and Danny frequently that they are a brotherhood now, equally committed, equally endangered by this plan. But what Shel doesn't realize is that the authoritative tone of his voice belies equality and that Jim responds to it with anger.

Now as they examine the sticks of dynamite, each wrapped in paper on which is written the warning NITROGLYCERIN HIGHLY INFLAMMABLE, each man is caught up in the thrill of this dangerous adventure.

Danny unloads his briefcase onto an old wooden table next to the box of dynamite: a large battery, a coil of wire, a simple wind-up alarm clock. He explains to the others the safest, most efficient way to wire up the bomb so that it will explode when they want it to. He holds up each piece and tells them how it will be used, what precautions must be taken to avoid danger to themselves. As he speaks, his soft voice with its Irish burr becomes more and more musical. He has grown up making such bombs, he has told them. Before he could read, he was helping the older boys snitch milk bottles from doorsteps in the streets of Derry in Northern Ireland to make Molotov cocktails.

"So, when will we wire it up?" Shel asks. Danny's careful explanations have not interested him. He is interested only in action.

"Thursday night. I'll put the bomb together, put it back into the briefcase. Before we do it. Right before. Once it's wired up, it's dangerous. Lethal."

The three of them nod respectfully. Shel is thinking that he's at a disadvantage. These two scientific men know more about such things than he does. He never trusts mechanical devices, which can behave unpredictably, fail to work when they're supposed to, or go off when they're not supposed to. He always feels he can't possibly know the ins and outs of such devices, all the things that can go wrong with them.

He's much more comfortable with ideas than things. It bothers him that things turn out to be so important for getting ideas across to people. Things like bombs, for example. He sighs deeply. The other two look at him, trying to gauge the meaning of his sigh. Again he feels the grave responsibility of being the leader of this undertaking.

"Let's go down to the Pub and drink on it," he says as Jim re-covers the dynamite crate.

Jim looks up, shocked. "But we can't be seen together," he protests.

"Of course not," Shel says. "You two go together. I'll go alone. We hardly know one another."

The three of them laugh. Whenever they have come near one another in public, they have exchanged nods and gone off in different directions. Jim and Danny are known to be friends. They are in related fields; Jim in chemistry and Danny in biochemistry. They have worked on joint experiments. But it is important that Shel, the one who has the reputation of being politically savvy, is not associated with either of them. "We'll lift a beer and catch one another's eye," Shel suggests.

Seated at the Pub bar, Shel picks up his mug and glances at the two men he has just left, seated at a table at the far end of the room, barely visible through the smoke. Shel swivels his stool around so that he is facing them. They are looking in his direction. They are picking up their mugs. He lifts his mug and drinks deeply. He likes this deception. It makes his heart pound faster, his blood race.

Over the rim of his mug he sees a tall, awkward figure making his way toward him across the room crammed with drinkers.

"Aw, Jesus," Shel mutters to himself, swiveling back to face the bar. But it's too late. The tall man is coming straight for him. His face in his mug, Shel feels the hand on his shoulder and he flinches. It is Lou Hammer, a big jerk, the dumbest of the English graduate students, possibly the dumbest graduate student who ever managed to get into a graduate school anywhere. And not just academically. This guy can't do anything right. His very presence is like a premonition of doom.

"Hi, Shel," the tall man says eagerly, in the voice of someone hoping the rebuff won't be too harsh. "How are ya, old buddy?"

"I'm just leaving," Shel says, finishing the last of his beer.

Lou ignores the insult, puts his face close to Shel's as he settles into an empty stool beside him. Shel is revolted by the weakness of that face, the nose, off-center, hooked like an anteater's, the futile chin. "I'd like to talk to you about my paper on Howells," Lou whispers confidentially.

"Look, Lou, I'm not interested in Howells. I've told you before. The whole period bores me."

"I'm not asking much," Lou begs. He is actually whining. "Maybe an hour of your time."

Suddenly Shel just wants Lou out of his sight. He has already ruined his good mood, interrupted the thrill of conspiracy. He doesn't want to look at that ugly face another second. "Come by my office next week. I'll see what I can do. I can't talk now."

Lou backs away finally. "Okay. I'll do that. Thanks, Shel. Thanks." He goes.

Shel orders another beer. Drinks it fast. Then he leans back against the bar assessing the people in the Pub. Jim and Danny are still there in the corner. But other than his two partners, he doesn't see anyone he knows. Mostly, they are undergrads out trying to escape from their books. At a table near the bar three coeds are seated. One of them is quite pretty, with the kind of silky blond hair he loves. He imagines how she will react to the bombing. Probably one of those rich little preppies from Greenwich or someplace who'll be scared shitless, who'll say it's the Commies. Shel feels his head floating like a large weightless balloon. Educating the overprivileged should be a part of the Movement, he thinks. He looks the girl over again. He'd love to go right up to her and start a conversation. Converting someone like her would be satisfying on many different levels.

Jim and Danny are moving toward the door. They do not look back at him.

He surveys the room again with satisfaction. Naturally, none of the stuffed-shirt English faculty are in the Pub. Or any of those fancy deans. Shel chuckles to himself as he imagines how they will react to the bombing. They'll curse like hell, but they'll admire the courage and intelligence of the person who was responsible. All over the country, thinking people will be encouraged to see that there are those who are taking the first step toward revolution, people who dare to attack the military-industrial state at its core. Blacks and whites, students and poor people, all the downtrodden will see that there are alternatives to the kind of military buildup going on in the United States right now. He can stop this immoral war, stop the killing, the napalming, the horror.

Shel's head is whirling with beer and power as he gets up and heads toward the door. Maybe he'll drop by Cindy Stevens's dorm, he thinks. Or maybe not. Keep 'em guessing. The best policy.

The blonde looks up at him as he passes near her. He smiles slowly, letting the smile spread. Flustered, she looks down at the table.

CHAPTER 5

Wednesday Morning, April 25, 1984

Lieutenant Cohen sat back in his desk chair and put his legs up on his wastebasket. The room was hot, and he'd slipped off his jacket and hung it over the back of his chair. All morning, as he interviewed people from Addison who had known Professor Silverman, reports had been arriving from the lab. He and Hughes had been reading them over as best they could between appointments. He had that feeling of being overwhelmed which he always had at the beginning of an investigation, when everything was up for grabs, but at least he wasn't sneezing this morning. The office was hot and airless. He began to roll up the sleeves of his Oxford blue shirt. Beside him, Hughes had already rolled up his sleeves and removed his tie.

"You know what I'd love right now?" Cohen asked.

"A Diet Pepsi," Hughes replied affably.

"I'm putting you up for promotion," Cohen joked as Hughes got lightly to his feet. Then Cohen returned to the reports on his desk.

In a few minutes Hughes was back with the icy can. "No word from Hammer?" he asked.

Cohen shook his head, reached for the drink.

"He's already fifteen minutes late," Hughes said.

"You surprised?" Cohen asked, then took a gulp.

"You?" Hughes countered.

Cohen put the can down on the desk. "I asked first," he said.

Hughes laughed good-naturedly. Cohen was always testing him, and he was always trying to come up with the right answer. He wasn't the brightest guy in the world, and he knew it. But he was learning. Yeah, he was learning. And he knew how lucky he was. If it wasn't for Cohen, he'd still be on the beat. And he knew if he didn't watch his step, he could be back there again. Cohen had given him the opportunity of a lifetime, choosing him for his assistant, and Hughes was determined to hold his own.

Cohen took another sip of his drink and thought that Hughes was the perfect aide: dying to please, not enough imagination to compete with him, yet enough of a sense of humor not to be a total bore. And there was something about his mediocrity that seemed to oil Cohen's investigative processes. Ah, he thought, as he put his feet back up on his wastebasket, at last I lucked into a decent assistant. In the five years that he had been a detective in Braeton specializing in homicide, this was the first assistant who had worked out.

Hughes checked his watch. "Seventeen minutes."

Cohen leaned back in his chair. "Let's use the time to summarize the reports that have been coming in this morning."

Hughes picked up the reports from Cohen's desk and reshuffled them carefully. He glanced up at Cohen, who was leaning way back in his swivel chair in a position of relaxation, eyes half-closed.

"Okay," Hughes began tentatively, scanning the sheets before him for the relevant information. "Time of death. Dr. Edman places it approximately between six and eight Monday evening, judging by body temperature and state of rigor. Cause of death. The bullet that penetrated the heart."

Cohen nodded.

"Multiple bullet wounds. Five. The bullets were copper-jacketed, from a twenty-two pistol. Not much to go on there." Hughes held up another sheet, studied it carefully. "The fingerprint experts really went to town in Silverman's office. Picked up dozens of prints, both visible and latent." Hughes's tone was critical.

"You think they overdid it?" Cohen asked.

Hughes shrugged. "Yeah. That Henry Becker is a little crazy for prints. Why'd they bother with so many prints? Only place they didn't find prints was on the empty coffee mug on his desk."

Cohen opened one eye.

Hughes went on, "That coffee mug on the desk—a plain white crockery one—belonged to Silverman. People said he used it for guests. He always drank out of the one that was broken on the floor, with the picture of the dove on it and his prints all over it. But the white mug on the desk was wiped clean."

Cohen opened both eyes, looked directly at Hughes. "So does that speak to you?"

Hughes caressed his chin with his index finger. "Whoever it was shot Silverman, he didn't want to leave his prints on the mug."

"He?"

"He or she didn't want to leave prints on the mug."

"What about gloves?" Cohen asked.

"Nah—I figure a social visit, cups of coffee. The murderer wouldn't tip his hand by wearing gloves."

"Fair enough," Cohen said. "So our murderer didn't mind leaving prints all over the place except on the mug. How come?"

"Maybe he managed not to touch anything but the mug."

Cohen smiled. "A very careful murderer. Well, maybe. But did you notice that I asked each of our interviewees this morning to tell us exactly what happened when he or she visited Silverman in his office? All of them—Professor Froming, Mrs. Waks, and Madeline Jennings-Ellison—said exactly the same thing. They would knock on the door. Silverman would call out, 'Come in.' He did not get up and open the door. Each one of them opened the door and entered, closing the door behind him. So, it seems likely that the murderer also had to open the door and close it behind him. We know that he didn't wipe his prints off the doorknob or anywhere else but the mug. So apparently he wasn't worried about leaving his prints anywhere except on the mug. Why not?"

Hughes studied the sheet from the fingerprint experts as if the answer could be found there. "Well, must've been somebody knew there'd be prints all over the place and so his—or hers—wouldn't give him—or her—away except on the mug."

"But why wouldn't the killer's prints give him away—except on the mug?" Cohen hammered.

Hughes looked at him blankly.

Cohen sighed, but Hughes could tell by his face that he wasn't displeased to have to come up with the answer himself. Cohen said, "The killer was someone whose prints would be in Silverman's office anyway, so he or she didn't have to wipe them away—except on the mug, as you say, where any prints would be those of the killer."

Hughes thought about that. Made sense. But he wasn't sure why it was so important. He thought, not for the first time, that his boss liked it better when his assistant didn't know all the answers. In fact, it occurred to Hughes, also not for the first time, that if he did know all the answers, he probably would've been transferred to another section by now.

Smiling, Cohen continued, "The killer was someone who entered Silverman's office as a matter of course, someone whose prints would be there anyway. An insider. Not an outside job. One of about two dozen or so faculty, staff, or graduate students, not to mention a dozen or so of his undergraduate students who have come in to see him since classes began. Edith Waks is working on lists for me."

Hughes was chagrined. It was obvious. Why hadn't he thought of it? "That's a lot of suspects," he said in a loud voice, trying to sound confident.

Cohen gave a short laugh. "We've got a big job here. But at least we can eliminate anyone who hasn't been up to his office in the past week or so."

"Why is that?" Hughes asked reluctantly.

"Because anyone who wasn't in there recently, very recently, couldn't have taken the chance that his fingerprints wouldn't show up on top of a dozen or so others in that room and alert us."

"I see," Hughes said sorrowfully. Missed again. "But you can't be sure about that."

"Not a hundred percent sure. No."

Hughes consulted his watch again. "Twenty-five minutes late," he said. "Shall I call the university? Hammer supposedly had a nine o'clock class this morning. Should've made it here easy."

Cohen nodded.

"And how about I turn the air conditioner on now?"

Cohen shook his head. "Not yet. Makes too much noise. Can't hear anything when it's going. We've only got a few more appointments this morning. Can you stand it?"

Hughes gave an exaggerated gasp. "Barely."

Cohen laughed. "Hughes, you're one in a million, to put up with closed windows in this hot spell to spare your boss's allergies. I tell you, you're indispensable."

Hughes perked right up. Gave Cohen that big beautiful grin.

"Tell you what," Cohen continued. "Go call Addison from the outer office while I look at these reports some more." Cohen removed his tie and threw it on the desk as he reread the ballistics report.

CHAPTER 6

Tuesday, April 30, 1968

On a rainy afternoon, the day before the bombing is scheduled, Shel is called into President Jarvis's office. The president claims that he has information—he will not say where it came from—that there is a conspiracy to carry out a destructive act at Page University. He emphasizes the word "conspiracy," a legal-sounding word, a dangerous word. Shel's name has been mentioned as being involved in this conspiracy.

Shel pounds his fist on President Jarvis's long teak desk, venting his frustration and fear in the name of righteous indignation. "Just because I am opposed to this immoral war in Indochina. Just because I am involved in antiwar protests doesn't mean I would consider harming Page in any way."

President Jarvis lifts his egg-shaped quartz paperweight and turns it around thoughtfully in the palm of his hand. "I hear that you are also opposed to Page's accepting defense contracts," he says.

Shel feels a flush starting at the back of his neck and moving up to his cheeks as the president approaches dangerous territory. He looks down at his hands resting on his knees, fingers touching the smooth cloth of his well-worn jeans like the claws of a bird poised for flight.

"If anything *should* happen, anything destructive, I would look to you," President Jarvis continues in his soft, precise voice, his hands still fondling the paperweight. "You are a leader here. Your words command attention." He is looking, not at Shel, but out the window behind Shel, out to his campus where the ground is patchy with the mud of early spring and the bare trees on the slopes are blackened by rain. Shel turns and follows his gaze to Lohr Science Center crowning the hill like a shrine of glass and steel.

Shel stands up and makes a great show of anger. "I am shocked at your accusations," he says, much more loudly than he intended. "I would never do anything to harm Page." In Shel's mind this is certainly the truth. He believes that by destroying the deadly experiment, he is helping, not harming, Page. He is going to make the university famous as the center of brave and enlightened opposition to the Vietnam War.

President Jarvis gives him an ironic smile. "Glad to hear it," he says, "because I will look very harshly on anyone who harms this university."

Shel is sweating profusely as he steps out of the president's office into the gray-carpeted, gray-walled waiting room and nods good-bye to Jarvis's prim, bespectacled secretary.

He cuts his afternoon seminar and walks alone around the campus. The early stirrings of spring—the tight, hard buds on trees and bushes, the few brave crocuses—disturb him deeply. That night he cannot sleep. Finally, as dawn begins to stain the sky, he dozes, only to awaken screaming from a dream of horror. He is falling into the crater of a volcano, catching on fire and burning as he falls, his legs churning

helplessly, his hands grabbing fire and air. He sits up gasping, fighting for breath. Although it is only six in the morning, he picks up the phone on his bedside table and calls Jim.

He hears the phone ring for a long time, ten, eleven
buzzes, and then Jim's sleep-numbed voice answers, low and
phlegmy. "Yeah, who is it?"

"Shel. I gotta talk to you."

"Jesus, Shel. It's not even morning. I'll call when I get
up."

"Now," Shel says.

The tall grass brushes against Shel's jeans, soaking right
through to his legs. He is sweating, even though the early-
morning air is cool. As he pushes through the undergrowth up
the slope to the meeting place behind the science center, he is
thinking hard. What he wants more than anything else, what
he has always wanted, is to be a professor of English, to write
critical works. To be recognized. He's already gotten a great
deal of encouragement from his professors. He has hopes that
the first three chapters of his dissertation on Walt Whitman
will soon be published in the form of an article. He is thinking
of the harsh realities of what will happen tomorrow morning
at 5 A.M., of splintered glass and crashing steel. For the first
time he is thinking beyond the moment of explosion.

All it would take would be a discreet note from President
Jarvis to ruin his chances of an academic appointment anywhere in the country. He reaches the cluster of trees and leans
against the black wet trunk of an oak, breathing heavily.
Without sleep, the climb up the slope has exhausted him. He
looks up the slope at the sweeping concrete expanse of the
rear of Lohr Science Center and he knows, now he knows for
sure, that he will pay for tonight's moment of triumph for a
long, long time. He jumps when Jim comes up behind him.

"Man, you're on edge," Jim says. "What's your problem?"

Shel looks at him for a moment, his heart pounding from the suddenness of his appearance. Shel sees him as if for the first time—a gangly, undernourished man, eyes close together peering out at a dangerous world, hostility always bubbling just below the surface of his high-strung personality. Shel is fully aware of Jim's need to best him, to best everyone. He sighs with the hopelessness of it and he begins. "Jarvis," he says in a hoarse whisper. "He's heard something. Called me into his office yesterday afternoon. Says if anything happens at Page he'll blame me. He knows something."

At first Jim says nothing. He just looks at Shel steadily from those close-together eyes. "He can't prove anything. He can't prove we're in it. And you sure couldn't do it yourself." Shel looks at the slight smile playing around Jim's lips. Jim enjoys watching him falter. This is what he's been waiting for.

Shel has always prided himself on being true to his beliefs, on standing up for what is right despite the consequences. He's still sure about what's right, but now he's worried. His career, everything he's worked for, could explode with that bomb.

Jim stands at ease, his lank brown hair fluttering in the morning breeze, assessing the chinks in Shel's armor. Jim is ambitious for himself, Shel knows. He'd like to be the leader of the revolution that is newly forming, that will soon sweep the country, the world, that will make the world a decent place to live in. Shel watches Jim's eyes spark with interest as he tries to figure out if this is his chance to nudge Shel out of his position of leadership, to take over.

Groggy from lack of sleep, Shel tries to formulate his suggestion in a way that will not discredit his leadership. But he knows he sounds weak as he says, "I think we should wait a little. Until the heat's off." Off me, he is thinking, and he senses that Jim knows what he is thinking. "The dynamite is safe in my basement. There's no need to rush this."

Even as he says it, he knows that Jim is immovable; he should have kept his worries to himself. Jim's face turns to stone. His blue eyes become as hard as marbles, his mouth firms into a line. "It's set," he hisses. Then he gives a forced laugh. "You're the one who keeps saying how the Movement is more important than any individual. And yet all Jarvis has to do is look at you cross-wise and you're in a panic."

"I'm thinking about the Movement, not about me," Shel says, and for the moment he believes it. "Our bombing should have all the power of surprise behind it. And it should seem like the work of a large cohesive group, not just a few dissidents."

"Then now *is* the time," Jim says quickly, interrupting him. "Right after the Columbia riots. Along with campus protests throughout the country and the growing antiwar movement. The time is now, all right. There is a Movement. Just like you've been telling us. And we're at the forefront." He finishes what is, for him, a long speech.

Shel knows he has lost the argument, knows that nothing will deter Jim. And there's no point in trying to talk to Danny. Odd as it seems to Shel, Danny looks up to Jim; he'll do whatever Jim tells him to do. Danny is both a born revolutionary and a follower. Jim's got him hell-bent for revolution and hell-bent he'll stay until Jim tells him otherwise.

Shel lets his eyes drift from Jim's to the building on the hill. "All right. All right." He turns and walks away from Jim's triumphant smile.

CHAPTER 7

Wednesday Noon, April 25, 1984

Cohen and Hughes sat at Cohen's desk talking in loud voices in order to hear each other above the whirring and clanking of the air conditioner. On top of the scattered papers on the desk lay Hughes's notebook in which he'd taken down in his cramped handwriting everything that had been said in the room that morning. Next to the notebook were two half-eaten hot pastrami sandwiches on waxed paper and two cans of Diet Pepsi with plastic straws. The room was still hot. The last interview of the morning had ended only twenty minutes ago and Hughes had turned on the air conditioner and gone out to get their lunch.

They chewed in silence for a while. Then Cohen leaned back in his chair and asked the younger man, "So, you think it could be Hammer killed the prof?"

Hughes licked crumbs from his fingers. "Could be," he said and gave a loud belch. He pointed to the corner of Cohen's sandwich in its waxed paper wrapping. "Uh, Lieutenant, you finished?"

"Go on, Tim, finish it if you want. I'm through." Watching Hughes eat, Cohen wondered, as he often did, how the young man could eat as much as he did and stay so thin, while he himself seemed to get fatter and fatter although he was eating less. At least he thought he was eating less. He patted his belly. That's about all he and Eva did for each other anymore. She cooked. He ate. When he tried to remember how it had been between them at first, it seemed like two other people he was thinking of. Twenty-nine years ago. He'd had a scholarship to Boston University. He'd dreamed of law school. Instead, he met Eva at Nantasket Beach the summer he worked as an auxiliary policeman and that was the end of that dream. There wasn't the money for both college and Eva. He'd joined the force.

When Hughes had polished off the rest of Cohen's sandwich, he threw their wrappings into the wastebasket and waited for orders.

"Summarize," Cohen said, stretching backward in his chair as if he were trying to touch the crown of his head to the floor.

"You mean about Hammer or all of them?" Hughes asked, ready to play it Cohen's way, but not quite sure what the older, more experienced man was thinking.

"Review all the testimony, the way we always do," Cohen said firmly, with an edge of criticism in his tone.

Flushed with annoyance at the implication that he didn't know his job well enough, Hughes hunched over his notebook and cleared his throat. "Okay," he began, "this morning we had Froming, Waks, Jennings-Ellison, then Hammer, who didn't show . . ." He looked up from his appointment sheet, but when Cohen made no comment, he looked down again and finished, "Davis, Applewhite, Reardon."

"Yes," Cohen said thoughtfully. "We've earned our pay this morning, that's for sure."

Hughes took one last noisy slurp of his soda. The can was empty.

"Finish mine, if you like," Cohen offered, eyes still closed.

Hughes finished his boss's soda. Then he began. Carefully. He knew Cohen considered these sessions as training, and that if he caught on fast, did well, he would be kept on. He felt he had a knack for criminal investigation and he suspected his boss thought so as well, although he never told him so directly. Hughes liked to picture himself in Cohen's job someday.

Taking a deep breath, he said, "First, Professor Ian Froming, chairman of the Department of English and Journalism, Addison University. Fifty-three years old, married, two grown children." He looked up, but Cohen just lay there in his flexible chair, as if asleep, so he continued. "A quiet, serious man, not big on emotion, seems to keep apart from the others."

"Froming heard shouting coming from Silverman's office late Monday afternoon. Uh, about . . . about five o'clock, maybe a little after. Froming's office is next to Silverman's. As Froming was leaving his office around 5:20, Silverman's door flew open and Hammer burst out, slamming the door behind him. He didn't speak to Froming, just hurried out of the building. Then Silverman came out of his office and Froming asked him if Hammer was all right. Silverman said Hammer was upset because he was worried about getting enough support at the tenure meeting in a few days. So Froming immediately clammed up because these tenure decisions are supposed to be confidential."

Hughes looked over at Cohen again. He could have been asleep. He pushed on. "Then you asked Froming about Hammer's chances for getting tenure. He answered that they

weren't good. Froming had a low opinion of Hammer's ability and his student evaluations were poor. But he had two
things going for him—first, a terrific book he'd written on
this poet . . ." Hughes squinted at the page, trying to read
his own writing. "Uh, Wallace Stevens, a book on him. And
second, Hammer had Silverman's support."

Cohen's eyes were open now. "And what did you think
Froming's attitude was toward Professor Silverman?" he
asked.

"I definitely had the feeling he didn't like the guy. But
what he said was . . ." Hughes found it on the page and
read, " 'I respected him as a teacher and a scholar, but didn't
agree with his political views.' "

"Which were?"

Hughes read on, " 'He was staging the antinukes rally at
Addison. He'd also taken a stand against United States in-
volvement in Central America, participated in that march on
Washington last spring to protest the U.S. taking sides in El
Salvador.' " Hughes shook his head. "All those hippies trying
to pretend it's the sixties again."

Cohen said, "Let's save your brilliant sociopolitical analysis
for another time and get on with it."

Unruffled, Hughes continued. "Let's see—opportunity.
Froming had it. All of the people we've talked to so far did.
We know Silverman died sometime between six and eight
Monday evening. None of the faculty, students, or staff was
in the building at that time, they say, yet none of them has
an airtight alibi either. Every blasted one of them, except
Applewhite, claims to have been in transit from somewheres
to somewheres else or in a place where no one would've remembered them. Froming was looking for a birthday present
for his wife at the mall. Claims it took an hour."

"What about motive for Froming?" Cohen coached.

"If there is one, it hasn't surfaced. You don't kill a guy because you don't agree with his politics."

Cohen closed his eyes again gently. He believed he thought best this way. With his eyes closed and the drone of Hughes's voice stating the obvious, he could allow his imagination to flicker over possibilities that were, perhaps, not so obvious. Somehow the very stolidity of Hughes's manner abetted Cohen's mood. "On to the next," he said.

Hughes ducked his head obediently into his notebook. "Edith Waks. That one loves to talk. Widowed eleven months ago. She went right home Monday afternoon at five o'clock because she had a headache. Lives in West Braeton, in the same house she lived in with her husband for thirty years. Took an aspirin, had a light dinner, went to bed with a novel."

"We don't have to hear everything. I know she told us what she ate before going to bed, too. What about her attitude toward the victim?"

"Of all of them, she's the only one who seemed to like him. They have dinner together sometimes—used to, I mean. She claimed he looked to her for advice, told her his problems, that kind of thing."

"Good. Let's hear the part about his problems."

Hughes was turning a page. "Here it is. Mrs. Waks said, 'He was incapable of satisfaction with one woman, always seeking affection from female figures.' "

Cohen interrupted, "She said that with a lot of affection herself. Affection and a few sniffles."

"You think Mrs. Waks could have been fooling around with him?" Hughes asked, astonished. "I mean, she's kinda old for that."

"The thought did cross my mind—at least, that she might've liked to have been." Hughes's eyes were popping. "However, I think it's more likely that she's the kind of woman who can get her satisfactions vicariously."

"Vicariously." Hughes tried out the word. "You mean by snooping into other people's lives?"

"Something like that." Cohen settled back in his chair. "Go on," he said.

"Okay. Mrs. Waks told us about a love affair between Professor Silverman and Madeline Jennings-Ellison. She said the affair started sometime last spring and went on until summer, at which time Silverman confided in her that he'd had to chuck Madeline because she'd gotten too demanding."

"And when was that?" Cohen asked.

Hughes studied his page. "August. Mrs. Waks explained that last summer Silverman took up with another young lady. He was still seeing that other young lady, a student named Chicky Manning, at the time of his death."

"That the one coming in this afternoon?"

Hughes nodded.

Cohen sat forward, resting both feet on the floor. "So, Mrs. Waks tells us Silverman told her *he* chucked Madeline. Yet, if I remember correctly, Madeline told us this morning that she was the chucker, he the chuckee."

Hughes was flipping pages eagerly. "Here it is. Madeline came in right after Mrs. Waks. When you asked her if she had been involved with Silverman, she didn't seem surprised that you knew. She said, 'Yes, it's true; I did have an intimate relationship with him through the spring and summer. But I broke it off when I realized that he was a phony. I hate to admit how foolish I was. But he had a line and I fell for it.'

"Then you asked her if she knew if he was seeing anyone

else while she was having this intimate relationship with him and she said that one thing she learned about him was that he was always seeing somebody else and always would. She said it in such an angry voice that you asked her if that made her angry with him, and she said angrily, 'Not at all—it makes me angry with myself for being such a fool.' "

Cohen leaned forward. "That was when I asked her if she knew about Silverman's seeing Chicky Manning."

"Yeah." Hughes scanned his notes. "She said, 'Chicky Manning—that did it, all right. A sophomore, for God's sake, and a dumb one at that. It took a Chicky Manning to make me see just what a stupid fool I had been. So I said to him, Get lost. And I came back to my senses.' "

The two men looked at each other. Cohen said, "So, we have a little discrepancy here. She says she ended it. He told Mrs. Waks he ended it."

Hughes said, "If he ended it and she didn't want it ended, she could've been real mad at him."

Cohen chuckled. "Hell has no fury like a woman scorned."

"Huh?"

"I was just agreeing with you. When do we have Ms. Manning?"

Hughes checked the sheet on which he had typed their afternoon appointments. "C. Manning 2:15 this afternoon."

"Good," Cohen said with satisfaction. He leaned back again and closed his eyes, motioning Hughes to continue.

Hughes turned another page. "Let's see, the next witness was supposed to be Professor Hammer, but he didn't show. When I called Addison, Mrs. Waks said he hadn't showed up for his nine o'clock or his twelve o'clock classes. I tried his home number and there was no answer. The next interview was with that graduate student Lisa Davis. There's something about her . . ." he trailed off thoughtfully.

"Oh, you mean she might be our killer?" Cohen asked, knowing exactly what Hughes meant.

"No," Hughes said, "I mean she's stacked."

"Stacked?"

"You know." Hughes gestured full circles with his hands.

"I know what stacked means," Cohen said. "What I don't know is what that has to do with our investigation."

A few months ago, Hughes might have thought he was serious. He knew his boss better now. He said with a straight face, "You told me yourself. A good investigator is aware that any fact might be relevant to his investigation."

Cohen sighed. "Don't you ever think of anything else?"

"Hardly ever," Hughes admitted.

Cohen leaned back again and said in a resigned tone, "Go on."

"Umm, Lisa Davis. Graduate student. Teaching Assistant in Silverman's class. Met with him every week to discuss the course—or so she said."

"Oh, you think she was lying?"

"Well, he was supposed to have been a womanizer. She's an attractive woman. Who knows what they did when they met?"

"All right, Hughes. Stop fantasizing and get on with it."

"Right. Lisa Davis said she met with Silverman every week to discuss the course, what he expected her to do and so on. Her attitude seemed to be that he was some sort of a joke. She said he ran after anything in skirts—jeans, I should say. Made a pass at her, but was easily discouraged. I certainly couldn't see anything like motive for murder in her statement. And she didn't seem to know anything about his personal life. Monday evening between six and seven she was jogging along the Charles River in Cambridge, near her apartment."

"Robert Applewhite came next. Graduate student who

works with Professor Froming. Shy, scared. No motive I can see. Hardly knew Silverman, or so he says. He's got the best alibi. He was in the library all evening Monday. Several people saw him during that time."

Cohen waved away Robert Applewhite.

"Last witness this morning," Hughes said, "was Professor Mary Reardon."

Now it was Cohen who showed appreciation, a long, low whistle.

"You think so?" Hughes asked in surprise. "A little too much of her, if you ask me."

"Just shows your lack of taste," Cohen said with a smile.

"Well, she's a lot of woman. And not a young chick."

"Possibly as old as thirty-five or -six," Cohen said.

"Yeah. Old," Hughes agreed, unaware of irony.

Cohen thought of the red-haired professor from Dublin, Ireland, who had said with her lilting voice and a flash of anger for the newly dead in her bronze eyes, "Naw, he wasna a verry nice man." She was a large woman, nearly six feet tall, with large soft curves. Her features were not beautiful, but had the kind of strength that Cohen had always admired. As Hughes read from his notes, Cohen wondered why he had wanted to marry Eva so badly. She had wrapped herself around him like an old woolen scarf. Must've aroused his protective instincts, he thought bitterly. If he had only known what a complainer she would become . . .

"So that's why Professor Reardon was in her office late."

"Uh, what'd you say?"

Hughes looked up from his notebook. "I said Professor Reardon had a late appointment with a student in her office, which abuts Silverman's office on the other side from Froming's. She said she heard shouting coming from Silverman's office. She and her student could hardly hear each other talk and she dismissed him. She couldn't hear what was being said in Silverman's office, but she could tell that the voices were men's. She recognized Silverman's voice and she thought Hammer's, although she said she couldn't swear to that."

"And her relationship with Silverman?" Cohen asked.

"She didn't know him all that well. She's only been here since the beginning of September, but she disliked his attitude toward women." Hughes read, " 'He was a hypocrite. He pretended to be a liberal, fair toward women, but it was only a pose.' He made a pass at her. She called him a . . ." Hughes was laughing. Cohen laughed, too, remembering what the fiery woman had said. "She called him a 'leprechaun-sized lecher,' and he didn't try again." Hughes paused and said thoughtfully, "He wasn't a small man, was he?"

Cohen was still laughing. "By her standards I guess he was."

"She also said," Hughes read, " 'He was one of those macho males who is really hiding his insecurity and sense of inferiority behind aggressive traits.' "

"All that and a psychologist, too," Cohen said. For a moment he imagined what it would be like explaining the details of the case to her once he'd solved it. She would be appreciative of his intelligence. Perhaps over dinner somewhere. Aw, Jeez, cut it out, you old chicken, he said to himself.

"No motive that I could see," Hughes was saying. "She was at home eating dinner between six-thirty and seven-thirty. She rents the home of a philosophy professor who is on sabbatical."

Cohen nodded. A woman like that eating dinner alone, he was thinking. What a waste.

CHAPTER 8

Wednesday Night, May 1, 1968

Shel feels a heaviness in his chest as he dresses in jeans and a black T-shirt. He tucks a flashlight in his pocket and turns out the light in his bedroom. In the darkness of his room, he looks out the window to the lake shining in the watery moonlight like a pewter plate. Tall black evergreens crowd around its rim.

Downstairs, in the basement, he waits until Danny arrives, alone as planned and right on time. With hardly a word between them, Danny quickly and efficiently fashions the bomb. Shel watches with a horrible fascination as Danny wires the dynamite sticks together with the nonchalance of a child constructing a Tinkertoy, and then hooks them up to the blasting cap, a small metallic cylinder.

"D'ya know the time?" Danny asks.

Shel glances at his watch and answers, "Ten to nine." Danny sets the small windup clock and pushes in the alarm button with a click. With rapid turns of the wires, he attaches the clock to the bundle of dynamite sticks. Shel feels his throat go dry, but Danny seems perfectly calm; he works efficiently in the same way that he would prepare an experiment in his lab.

When he has finished wiring the bomb, he puts it in the old briefcase that Jim found in a trash bin downtown weeks ago. Danny's coolness amazes Shel, who feels as if his brain is about to explode right through the top of his head. His hands are shaking so that he could never put a bomb together, even if he knew how, he thinks, as he opens the basement door for Danny. He watches the muscular young man cross his backyard and head into the woods from which he will make his circuitous journey to the slope behind Lohr Science Center.

Shel locks the door behind Danny. Back upstairs he takes a drink of water at the kitchen sink. He stands at the window looking out at the lake much longer than he should. Then he leaves his cottage by the front door and walks beside the lake toward the main campus.

On the outskirts of the campus, he passes a fraternity house, an old mansion that has seen better days. Beyond its sagging porch and splintered columns, he can see through a tall front window into a brightly lighted room. A party is in progress. Maybe a party is always in progress. Boys raise bottles of beer to their lips, tipping their heads back. A small-hipped girl in jeans is dancing. She is either stoned or very, very loose; her shoulders and hips move as if they are fluid, her long dark hair flows and swirls like underwater weeds. Shel longs to walk in through the open front door and dance with her. He'd like to feel nothing but the beat of the music and the answering rhythms of his body. He hurries past the frat house, slips in among the trees, and starts the long climb up the hill.

Jim and Danny are waiting in the tangle of bushes behind the science center. Danny is leaning against a tree, his body another ambiguous shape in the darkness. But Jim is pacing, giving off sparks of heightened energy. "You're here," he says accusingly as Shel nears them. "What took you so long?"

Again, Shel is aware of the shift in the balance of power. Instead of answering, he looks over at Danny, who unbends his muscular body and leans toward Jim out of the darkness. Danny says nothing. The briefcase is at his feet, resting against his leg. Shel can hardly look at it.

"Let's go," Shel says in an even voice, ignoring Jim's challenge.

They push up the hill until they are standing in the clump of evergreens behind the science center. From here they can see the concrete mass of the building looming above them and the walk leading up to it. They can see Hill Hall, the old building next to Lohr, and they can look across the dark grassy quadrangle to the lighted windows of Jackson Hall.

This part of the campus is deserted. Except for the few lighted windows in the three buildings, there is no sign of activity. They wait. The moon pops out between the gathering clouds and hangs there for a while. Danny takes a joint out of his pocket and holds it up. Both Jim and Shel shake their heads. In the greenish moonlight Danny's face looks like that of a kid who didn't get a prize at a birthday party. Does he even understand that the light of a joint could give them away? Shel wonders. This boy, who is such a whiz at science and in all other respects such a booby, would be happy to die on the barricades, Shel realizes. He's a natural revolutionary: committed to action, he does not think. Shel feels a shiver course through his body, and he recognizes it for what it is— fear. He looks up at the moon, pale and watery, bloated, as if it is about to shed tears. It is cold, and now there is a steady but light drizzle. Shel shivers again.

After a while, the side door of Jackson Hall, the large old stone building across the quad from Lohr, opens with a metallic creaking. A figure steps out under the light above the door. Harry McVey, the night watchman. The door shuts behind him with a loud clang, and McVey walks at an easy pace toward Lohr along the dirt path, the keys on his belt clashing in the quiet night. The three men watch him sort through his keys on the steps of the science center. As he unlocks the front door the chapel bell below in the South Quad sends forth its slightly tinny chimes. They seem to go on forever. Twelve of them. Twelve o'clock.

While McVey is inside Lohr, Shel sees a window darken suddenly. It is the window of the lab that has the secret Defense Department contract. A few minutes later McVey and another man come out of the building. McVey jiggles the doorknob to make sure it is locked. Satisfied, he walks along beside his companion, who is a full head taller than he is and much broader. Shel recognizes the large man pulling on his sweater as he walks. Anthony Budlong, reputedly working on the secret Defense contract for Clinton Chemical Corporation, developing the substance that is like napalm, but a hundred times more lethal. What kind of man would do such work?

The two men walk down the path. Their voices drift back, McVey's burred with a gentle Scottish accent. "And I didna plant the tomato seeds outside until May and yet . . ."

They stand for a moment at the crossing of two paths, and Budlong's voice, clipped and precise, very Yankee, splits the air. "Bone meal. With bone meal I have never had a failure," he insists, drowning out the gentler voice. Failure, clearly, is something this man would never tolerate. The two men part.

Budlong takes the path that turns off to the parking lot; Mc-Vey walks straight, down the hill toward the south campus.

Shel looks up at Lohr. Three windows are still lighted. He wipes the back of his hand across his upper lip. He hopes they'll stay in there all night. It's been known to happen. "Who's in there?" he whispers to Jim. "Those are the bio labs," Jim answers.

And Danny pipes up, "Harrison's rats."

Shel tries once more. "Maybe we should just skip it."

Jim is ready for him. "It's *your* plan, for Christsake."

And even as he says it, as if by a prearranged signal, a light goes off, then another. They wait, all staring, heads tilted upward until the third window is blackened. In a few moments three men walk out of the building together.

"That's Sam," Danny whispers.

Sam Harrison is flanked by the two other men. They stand for a few minutes in front of the building, under the light. Harrison is overweight, with thick unruly dark hair. The others are younger, leaner. They are all talking together with enthusiasm. Harrison seems to need his hands to talk.

"Of all the times for the centrifuge to conk out," one of the young men exclaims.

"It'll be fixed. A few more days won't ruin us," Harrison says. There is a calm humor in his tone that is soothing.

"Just a few more days," the other young man repeats in a high, excited voice. "The longer we let the virus particles develop on the isolated cell, the better."

"Engineering promised that Peter would be down to take a look at it no later than ten tomorrow," Harrison says.

They disappear down the path to the parking lot, their voices trailing behind them. It is raining lightly but steadily now. Lohr is in blackness. The other buildings, too, are dark. Only the lights above the doorways of Lohr and Jackson are visible, wavery and blurred in the rain. In the silence Shel imagines he can hear the alarm clock ticking like muffled heartbeats in the briefcase at Danny's feet. He thinks of Poe's "Telltale Heart" and shivers.

Jim, Danny, and Shel glide through the trees toward Lohr. In the shrubbery next to the main entrance Jim turns to Shel, as if he must remind him. "Remember. If anyone should come, you head him off with that story about noises in Hill."

Shel suppresses an angry retort at Jim's takeover tone. He is aware that he has relinquished his leadership and that Jim is in control now. He stays in the shrubbery as the other two walk quickly toward the building.

From his vantage point he can see Jim unlock the front door with his key. The two of them slip inside and the door clicks softly behind them. Shel is left standing alone. A breeze sways the pine boughs and shadows move toward him like accusing figures. He takes a deep gulp of pine-scented air. His hands are shaking. His throat feels constricted. He can hardly swallow. He seems to hear President Jarvis's words in the sighing pine branches: "If anything should happen, I would look to you . . ." The mass of Lohr Science Center threatens him with stern authority. He paces between the dark bushes. He tries to will his body to relax.

The rain is heavier now. He stands under a pine tree, but he is still getting soaked. Suddenly he hears a soft whistle coming from the direction of South Quad. The whistle is rich, throaty. Shel hears in his head the words that go to the tune, "By yon bonny banks and by yon bonny braes . . ." Loch Lomond. The whistling grows louder. Jesus Christ, Shel whispers, as Harry McVey's short, wiry form appears, now moving lithely up the path. Why the hell is he back so soon? They have clocked McVey's activities for weeks, and in all that time the man has spent at least ten or fifteen minutes every night making the rounds. But it is raining tonight. It is really raining. They hadn't planned for rain in their calculations. Rain had never even occurred to them. Shel is soaking wet. And that little man, hurrying, nearly at a run, up the path right toward him must be soaking wet also. He must have shortened his rounds because of the rain.

Hunched into his jacket, feeling cold and wet, Shel watches McVey approach. With luck he'll head for the room he uses as a guard station in Jackson Hall across the quad, where he has a view down the hill toward South Quad. He'll sit there in the window nursing his coffee for a while before starting all over again on his rounds.

Shel stands perfectly still. Rain from a pine branch drips down the back of his collar and he moves slightly, soundlessly as he watches McVey running up the path. The watchman approaches the intersection of the paths. If he continues straight ahead, he will be heading directly toward Lohr Science Center. The right fork leads to Jackson Hall and his watchroom, the left fork to Hill Hall.

Still whistling, McVey halts at the intersection of the paths, a dark shadow facing the front of Lohr. Then he takes a step in the direction of Jackson Hall.

Shel lets his breath out in an explosion of relief. He hadn't even realized he'd been holding it.

But wait! McVey suddenly stops whistling, jerks his body around toward Lohr. Snaps his head back in a kind of doubletake. He has seen something. In the moment that his eyes flickered over the building as he took a step toward Jackson Hall, something has alerted him to trouble. He stands like a statue hewn of black marble in the center of the path, facing Lohr, facing Shel. Shel instinctively backs up farther into the shadows.

Dammit, McVey must have seen the ghost of a flashlight beam. Maybe those jerks didn't pull the shades down. Or it could be that there's a gap between the bottom of the shade and the window frame. Or maybe it was only instinct that alerted the old man.

Shel watches as McVey's body remains alert; he steps back from the side path, back into the intersection of the paths, looking straight at Lohr, his chin tilted upward, his head turning slightly from side to side as his eyes sweep the upper stories. Then the watchman makes his decision. He starts walking quickly toward Lohr.

Shel crouches down and backs farther into the wet bushes. He knows what he's supposed to do; he's supposed to scramble down the hill through the bushes and when he meets McVey on the path, pretend he is rushing toward him from Hill Hall to tell him that he has seen someone moving around in the lobby through the huge plate-glass front doors of the building. Shel and McVey will then enter Hill together, check the priceless rare books and holographs in the glass cases of the first-floor lobby.

By the time he and McVey investigate and return to Lohr, Jim and Danny will be finished with their task and safely out of the building. The bomb will be deposited in the corner of the laboratory in the old leather briefcase that would never be noticed among the boxes of equipment and file cabinets in the corner. It will tick relentlessly until 5 A.M., when the daytime guard will arrive to relieve McVey and the two men are having a cup of coffee together in the Jackson guard room before the day watchman begins his tour of duty.

That was the plan. Now, as Shel shivers and curses in the bushes, he sees the whole situation in a different light. No matter how honest and innocent his dealings with McVey appear tonight, when the bomb goes off at five in the morning, destroying the laboratory in which it was placed and God knows what else, his decoy role will become patently clear. He knows that now.

Why was I so stupid not to know it before? he asks himself. And he realizes that he never thought he would have to carry out the plan. It had seemed so unlikely that the watchman would depart from the schedule he had followed for weeks that Shel had never thought through the effect of his being a decoy. But now that he is thinking it through, he understands that as soon as his name is mentioned by McVey in his reconstruction of what went on tonight, Jarvis will be on him like a tick on a rabbit. Jarvis will make sure that he can't get a job at any university in the country. And he'll bring criminal charges against him for destroying university property. As if for the first time, Shel tries to assess the amount of the damages that will result from the bomb. Millions, he thinks, as he shivers in the rain.

McVey is walking rapidly toward him. In the light at the front of the building, Shel can see the old man's sagging cheeks, his nose, prominent and veiny. Rumor has it that McVey imbibes more than coffee in the Jackson guard room.

Now, Shel thinks, now, he should run toward the old man, feigning worry, concern for Page's precious books. He hears the phrases he should speak in his head. I was just passing on my way to the library. I thought I heard glass breaking. The rare books. The holographs. Now. Now. His muscles tense. But instead of rushing to McVey, he backs stealthily down the hill. Slowly. Carefully. The soggy branches bend to allow his body passage but do not creak or break. The darkness and wetness conspire to protect him as he works his way silently down the hill behind Lohr Science Center. Past the place where he had met the others earlier.

Even though he can no longer see the watchman, Shel hears the sounds of his shoes on the concrete stairs of the building, like the beats of a drum. His key grinds in the lock. The door slams shut behind him, and Shel is encompassed in silence like that of the end of the world as he continues his slow descent through the thick, wet brush.

He hears the explosion when he is almost at the bottom of the hill, but he can see nothing through the trees. He looks all around, eyes wide with fear. Then he begins to run fast, gasping, plowing through branches; he falls, his chest heaving. He runs, his heart a painful, throbbing wound in his chest.

CHAPTER 9

Wednesday Afternoon, April 25, 1984

Cohen leaned way back in his chair and put his feet up on the clutter of papers on his desk, his hands clasped behind his neck. "So, now, who would want to shoot up a somewhat radical, on-the-far-side-of-young college professor? And not just kill him, don't forget. Our murderer hurt him real bad before he blew him away. Five bullet holes. Made him suffer before he shot him in the heart." He looked over at his assistant through slitted eyes, pleased as the faint flush began on Hughes's neck, spreading quickly to cover his high cheekbones. Hughes knew he was being tested. Cohen loved the power he had over his ambitious, hardworking, moderately bright, but unimaginative assistant. It made up a little for his spreading paunch, his middle-aged nearsightedness, his lousy marriage to shake up this good-looking young man who was so free that he didn't even have a steady girlfriend, never mind a wife and kids to support.

Hughes began, as he was expected to, trying to sound sure of himself, but stuttering a little over his words in his eagerness to impress Cohen. "Well, first of all, there's Professor Louis Hammer," he suggested, taking his pencil out of his mouth. He relaxed his lean body into the straight wooden chair as best he could, playing the question-and-answer game the way he hoped his superior wanted him to. "Both Professor Froming and Professor Reardon stated that they heard an argument Monday afternoon between the two of them, and it wasn't the first time they'd overheard an argument between them. Then, Silverman is murdered soon after. Figures his murder might have something to do with that argument."

"Hmnn." Cohen managed to look reflective with his eyes closed. "So, what do we know about that argument? What do we know about the relationship between Silverman and Hammer?"

Hughes flipped pages back and forth. "Here. Here's something, something Professor Reardon said when you asked her what she knew about their relationship." He read from his notes, unconsciously lilting his voice in imitation of hers. " 'Professor Hammer and Professor Silverman had a very close relationship. Yet it seemed to be without warmth.' " Hughes looked up briefly, saw Cohen's eyes on him, went on. "Then, you asked her if she thought they disliked each other and her eyes kinda caught on fire and she said, 'I don't know. I never thought of that, but maybe so.' "

"So, a close relationship, yet maybe they disliked each other. Interesting contradiction." Cohen blew his nose. "Anything else?"

"Well, we heard that Hammer was worried about getting enough of the professors to vote for him to get tenure." Hughes looked up, his forehead creased.

"Go on."

"Maybe Hammer was afraid Silverman wasn't going to support him?" Hughes looked steadily, hopefully at his superior.

It was a reasonable guess. "Or wasn't going to support him

enough," Cohen amended. He began to rock backward in his chair. He thought, harsh words, shouting. Hammer bursts out of Silverman's office angrily. Silverman tells Froming that Hammer was upset about the tenure vote. One could certainly guess that Hammer had come to Silverman's office to ask for something he felt entitled to, maybe something he thought Silverman owed him, and then became angry because Silverman wouldn't give him what he wanted. But what was it? His support? Would Hammer kill Silverman because of a tenure vote? Not unless the man were completely unbalanced.

Hughes's head was bowed over his notes.

"None of the people we interviewed seemed to like our victim much, except for Mrs. Waks. Would you agree, Hughes?"

Hughes nodded. "They all seem to think that he was very smart, did his job okay. Froming said he didn't like his politics. That graduate student Applewhite said he was considered pompous by the students. Lisa Davis thought he was a great brain but a zero on the social side. And Professor Reardon said he was the kind of man who mentally undressed every broad he looked at."

Cohen laughed. "Watch your language, Hughes."

"I didn't say nothing dirty. I just repeated what that broad said."

"Broad's the dirty word, Hughes. I'll bet a word like that around the Addison English and Journalism Department would get you a whack on the head with a *Complete Shakespeare*."

"Speaking of broads," Hughes said, "there's Madeline Jennings-Ellison. Another good looker. If Silverman ditched her like Mrs. Waks said, she could've been real mad."

"Mad, eh?" Cohen smiled. "Mad enough to murder?"

"But why would she do it now?" Hughes asked. "They broke up last summer."

Cohen shrugged.

Hughes was thoughtful. "I like Hammer for the murderer better than Madeline. What do you think?"

Cohen swung his legs onto the floor. "I think it's time to see if we can find Professor Louis Hammer. I have a feeling he'll have some answers for us."

CHAPTER 10

Wednesday Night, May 1, 1968

As he nears the bottom of the hill, Shel hears another explosion, louder than the first. An acrid smell, like old rubber burning, drifts toward him. He looks back, up to the top of the hill, and now he can see above the treetops the dark sky marked by an even darker tracing of thin black smoke curling like skywriting. In the moment that he watches, the smoke wafts higher, thins out, disappears into the blackness of sky.

He runs again, faster, through a shallow brook, splashing icy water on his jeans. His feet are soaked through his sneakers, but he runs on, gripped by a panic that fills his body with such purpose that he barely notices his discomfort.

He crashes through the brush and onto the road. On the other side of the road, he runs across a cleared field, damp and marshy with spring rain. His breath is coming in short gasps. The pain in his chest is almost unendurable. But he doesn't let up. Ahead in the misty blackness he can make out the outlines of several buildings that back up to the farmland—a large farmhouse, a barn, and several smaller structures. All dark and silent. He heads toward a small cottage behind the barn.

He stands by a slightly open window, trying to catch his breath. Finally he says, "Lou," in a tortured whisper. He stands near the window, drawing ragged breaths. Rain drips steadily over the gutters and splashes onto the mud below. "Lou," he calls more loudly. "Lou."

At last he hears sounds from inside. A groan. The creaking of bedsprings. A voice jolted out of sleep. "What?"

"Lou," Shel says again.

"Who?" A scuffling sound. Feet on floorboards. Lou's astonished face appears in the window.

"Are you alone?" Shel demands, still in a whisper.

"Shel? That you?"

"Are you alone?" Shel repeats.

Lou looks around as if to make sure. He nods.

"Lou, I need help." The desperation is there, in his voice.

CHAPTER 11

Wednesday Afternoon, April 25, 1984

The air was damp with the warm heavy odor of wet earth as Lieutenant Cohen and Officer Hughes drove to the section of Braeton near the railroad station where garden apartments had sprung up like houses on a Monopoly board. As they drove up Depot Street, Cohen was seized by paroxysms of sneezing, which made him jump and twist in his seat as if he were having a fit. Hughes, alarmed, pulled over to the curb.

"What the hell you stopping for?" Cohen yelled.

"I thought . . . you all right?"

" 'Course I'm all right. You never heard anyone sneeze before? Jesus, close your window. Those goddamned budding trees. Never used to bother me."

The two men rolled up the windows and drove in silence in the sweltering car waiting for the air conditioning to take effect. Concerned, Hughes glanced over at Cohen, who was still wiping his nose. At least he had stopped sneezing.

"That's the one. The one on the right," Cohen said as they approached some low brick buildings arranged symmetrically around a central courtyard of grass with crocuses and yellow tulips blooming along the borders. "Yeah," Cohen said as

Hughes drove closer, "that first building is ninety-three. The next must be ninety-five."

Hughes parked the car, and the two men walked up the central pathway. The buildings were mock-Colonial with white columns recessed into their brick facades and white shutters at the windows. A central building parallel to the street was flanked by two buildings facing each other. The central building had a bronze 95 above the front door.

"Whaddya wanna bet he ain't here," Hughes said as he pressed the button under the mailbox marked HAMMER 2-D in the vestibule. He rang several times, his other hand on the doorknob ready to turn in reply to the buzz.

A young woman with short-cropped hair carrying a book bag opened the door from the inside and started out. She looked at Hughes suspiciously as he grabbed the door from her and held it open with his shoulder.

Cohen took his ID out of his pocket and held it out to her. "Lieutenant Cohen of the Braeton police."

The girl studied the ID card for a moment. "Yes?" she asked impatiently.

"We've been ringing Professor Hammer's bell and we get no answer. Would you know if he's in?"

She shook her head. "I don't know. He's at the other end of the hall from me. Upstairs." She pointed.

"Could you tell me if there's a custodian in the building?"

"Yes. Super lives at ninety-three. In the basement."

"Thanks," Cohen said. He and Hughes walked up the open metal staircase to the second floor of the apartment building and knocked several times on the door of 2-D. No answer.

The super, Mr. Costello, was just starting to eat lunch when they rapped on his door. "It'll just take a moment," Cohen promised the hawkfaced old man, who seemed annoyed at the interruption.

The three of them climbed up the stairs, old Mr. Costello breathing heavily to show how put out he was. When he reached 2-D he knocked on the door.

"We already tried that," Cohen said.

"Invasion of privacy," Mr. Costello muttered, but he jiggled his keys until he found the right one. The door swung inward and Cohen stepped in first with long paces, across a worn moss-green square of carpet. Near the kitchen alcove stood a blond wood dining table piled high with mail mixed with stacks of papers and books. Cohen glanced into the kitchen—messy but not disgustingly so. Some dirty plates and silver filled the top of a tiny stacking table, a napkin was balled up on the white, flecked linoleum floor. An open cabinet door above the sink revealed assorted dishes and glasses. Cohen turned in the opposite direction and walked down the hallway.

Hughes still stood next to Mr. Costello near the open apartment door.

"Shoulda asked to see your search warrant," Costello muttered. Then taking two paces into the room, he shouted in the direction Cohen had taken, "You got a search warrant?"

"Won't be necessary," Cohen said, reappearing suddenly. His face looked grim. "We're investigating a suspicious death. Don't touch anything."

Both Hughes and Mr. Costello stared at him, eyes wide with surprise.

"I'll stay here," Cohen said to Hughes. "You go back with Mr. Costello. Call the medical examiner and the crime lab from his place. Get Mr. Costello's statement."

Hughes started to move toward the door, feeling slightly annoyed that Cohen felt he had to spell out exactly what to do.

"Oh, take a look first," Cohen said, as if he knew what Hughes was thinking. "I'll want to pick your brain when we get back. First door on your right. I'm especially interested in your views on what's next to the typewriter."

Hughes walked down the short hallway covered by a narrow strip of the same green carpet. Ahead was a closed door. Bathroom? To his right the door was open. He walked into the room, careful not to touch anything as he had been trained. His eye was caught instantly by the still figure.

The man was lying sprawled on the wooden floor, his head, turned away from the doorway, resting on a small braided rug. He lay like a swimmer doing the crawl, one arm above his head, one down by his side. His legs also were positioned as if he were about to move, to kick down with one leg and raise the other, as if he had dropped to the floor suddenly while in motion. Between his white T-shirt and his jeans a band of skin was exposed, with a line of dark, feathery hair growing up the center of his back from his belt. The hair looked so alive that Hughes felt like reaching out and touching it.

It was only when he moved up close to the body and knelt down beside it that Hughes could see the neat hole in the temple and the blood that had soaked into the braided rug. He also saw the revolver clutched in his hand, his right hand, the hand that was thrown out as if about to take a swimmer's stroke.

Hughes touched the man's bare forearm just below the shirt sleeve. It was cold. As cold as the dead. He walked over to the desk on which stood a portable Smith-Corona typewriter and next to it a sheet of typewriter paper on which a note was neatly typed with careful attention to spacing and margins.

Hughes leaned over the desk and read:

> I shot Professor Sheldon Silverman, and I now shall do the same for myself. In my judgement Silverman deserved to die. He was the murderer of three. I have protected him all these years, but I can no longer endure the empty lie my life has become.

The letter was signed in ink, "Louis Jason Hammer." A ballpoint pen, gray with a red cover, lay neatly beside the note on the desk.

Hughes breathed softly to himself, "So that's it."

CHAPTER 12

Wednesday Night, May 1, 1968

Shel stands shivering at Lou Hammer's front door, hunched into his jeans jacket. He glances behind him and all around him as he waits. No lights. No sounds. Nothing but the black dripping night, the empty stretch of farmland, the silent farm buildings.

At last the cottage door opens. Lou Hammer stands there like a little boy in red-and-white striped pajamas. Frightened. Innocent. It is Lou's innocence that makes Shel lose control. His sobs are deep, racking shudders that jolt his body like spasms of pain.

Lou takes his arm and pulls him in. "Shel, Shel," he intones sadly, astonished to see this man whom he admires above all men so shaken. Shel allows himself to be drawn inside. "You're soaked," Lou says. "Here. Let me get you some dry clothes."

"Lou," Shel gasps. His breathing is still painful, his heart is pounding, he is still shuddering. "I need your help."

CHAPTER 13

Wednesday Afternoon, April 25, 1984

"Come in," Cohen said, as he pushed the sheaf of papers off to one side of his desk and half-rose from his chair.

The girl who stood uncertainly in the doorway had one of those beautiful childlike faces with wide-spaced eyes and a small, pouting mouth. Her straight dark hair hung to her waist. Her clothes, blue T-shirt and jeans, clung to her slim figure as if they were wet.

"Sorry to keep you waiting, but something unexpected has come up." Cohen did not say what it was. He had decided to continue the interviews as scheduled and not announce Hammer's death publicly until after the postmortem and the other lab reports were in.

Cohen motioned the girl into the seat across the desk. "I'm Lieutenant Cohen and this is my assistant, Officer Hughes."

Cohen observed the long moment of eye contact between his assistant and the young woman. He felt a wave of dyspepsia. So much for hot pastrami. His head was stuffed again, too. He looked down at the sheet of paper in front of him. Charlotte Manning, daughter of a Scarsdale jeweler.

"Ehmmn," he cleared his throat loudly and the girl's eyes

snapped away from Hughes's to meet his. "Charlotte," he began.

"Chicky," she corrected in a voice he couldn't believe, high and squeaky, yet self-assured, a confident Mickey Mouse voice.

"Chicky, then." He glanced over at Hughes who was looking down at his notebook, suppressing a smile. "We want to talk to you about Professor Sheldon Silverman."

"What do you want to know?" Instantly cooperative in that astounding voice.

Cohen evaluated her expression. Sincere. Or so she seemed. Certainly no anguish at her loss evident. He leaned back in his chair. "Why don't you tell us in your own words about your relationship with Professor Silverman. Start at the beginning—how you met him."

Chicky seemed completely at ease as she began. "I didn't actually meet Shel until last summer, when I took his journalism course." She looked straight at Cohen as she spoke, giving Hughes only an occasional glance, as if to make sure he was getting it all down. "Oh, I'd seen him around all last year when I was a freshman, and he'd always given me the eye, you know, but we never spoke or anything." Her voice had veered from self-confident to self-important as her story unfolded. Then, abruptly, she stopped talking and started rummaging around in her purse. She came up with a crumpled package of Winstons. "D'ya mind?" she asked.

"Very much," Cohen answered. "I'm allergic and cigarette smoke is the worst."

Surprised and a bit embarrassed, she fumbled the cigarette package back into her bag.

"Please go on," Cohen prodded.

She looked over at Hughes, who gave her his winning

smile. She returned the smile and seemed to relax again. "I decided to go to summer school to get my science requirement over with. See, I flunked it—math. I took it for my sci requirement and, well, I can't *do* math. Shouldn't have taken it. Anyway, I didn't want to have to louse up my sophomore schedule, so I decided to take Rocks for Jocks summer session."

"*What* did you take?"

"Geology for nonscience majors."

"Uh, *huh*."

"And I decided, since I was going to summer school anyways, I might as well take a course I wanted. So I took Shel's History of Journalism. I'm a journalism major."

"And that's where you met Professor Silverman, in his course?" Cohen asked.

"No. My friend Nancy had been seeing him. I met him at her place."

"Nancy had been seeing him? You mean going with him?"

Chicky shook her head impatiently. "No. She wasn't *going* with him. She was *seeing* him."

"I don't think I understand the difference between those terms," Cohen said. Out of the corner of his eye he saw Hughes, head down over his notebook, trying not to laugh.

Chicky sighed and explained, "Going with someone implies a commitment, a sense that this is it."

"And seeing someone is just . . . seeing someone?"

"That's right."

"Does seeing someone mean sleeping with someone?"

Chicky was shocked. "I don't think that's any of your business."

"I'm investigating a murder here," he stated flatly. He thought, but did not say, At least one.

"I don't see . . ." she began. Her high, offended voice making her sound like an angry bird.

Cohen stampeded right through it. "Silverman's habits, the nature of his love affairs, any of that might tell us something."

She nodded, accepting his authority, but continued carefully. "I knew Nancy was just seeing him. He took her out for dinner sometimes. They slept together sometimes. Casual. Nancy told me Shel saw other women, too." She paused. She seemed to be waiting for Cohen to comment.

"Go on," he said.

"The day I met him, it was late afternoon and he'd come back to Nancy's place for a beer after class. I just kinda dropped in; I didn't know anyone was there. He recognized me from class, even though it was a big lecture and we'd only had a coupla meetings so far, and I knew he was interested."

"How did you know?"

Chicky looked at him sharply to see if he was kidding. When she saw he wasn't, she answered seriously, "He kept looking at me and making remarks."

"Do you remember any of the remarks?"

"Well, let me think." She thought hard. "He said, 'Uh, Addison's taste in students is improving.' And then when Nancy was on the phone, he was asking me my opinions about *Middlemarch*, which I had just finished reading for World Lit, and he said he'd like to 'touch my mind.' *That* interested me very much. Because lotsa guys have wanted to touch my body. But my mind! That was something else."

"Yes," Cohen said thoughtfully. Chicky had a spiritual glow in her eyes, just thinking about Silverman's remark. Hughes was staring at her. Cohen couldn't tell what he was thinking, but he could guess. "And did he?" Cohen asked.

"Did he what?"

"Touch your mind?"

"Oh." Chicky sighed. "Yes. He did. Being with him was like no one I've ever been with before. We talked about such interesting stuff. And, it was true, he *was* interested in my mind, not just my body. Although he was good in bed, too—for a guy his age—very good. And he never got possessive. He didn't care that I was seeing other guys, too. We never put each other through that. Never cared or asked what the other one was doing when we weren't together."

Chicky's face darkened for an instant. And Cohen wondered if she were thinking what he was thinking, about how much disease could be passed back and forth that way. But then she said, "Last summer Shel had this girlfriend and she acted so possessive." Chicky shook her lovely head in dismay at the very thought of such unpleasant behavior.

"Whoa. What's this about Shel having another girlfriend? I thought you were his girlfriend—after your friend Nancy," Cohen said, pretending to be confused.

"I told you," Chicky said impatiently, her voice a squeak, "I wasn't going with him, I was just seeing him."

"Right. You did tell me. And this girlfriend, what was her name?"

"Madeline. She's a graduate student. Two last names."

"Jennings-Ellison?"

"Yeah." Chicky looked surprised, and Cohen could tell she was thinking, Why are you asking me all these dumb questions if you already know the answers?

"Madeline Jennings-Ellison. Was she going with Shel?"

"Sort of."

"And when Shel started seeing you last summer, she didn't like it?"

"That's putting it mildly."

"What did she do?"

"God—what didn't she do? Screamed. Threatened. You name it."

"So, if I understand you correctly, Madeline became very upset when she found out that Shel was seeing you because she was, or thought she was, his girlfriend at the time."

"That's right," Chicky said, pleased that he'd gotten it straight.

"And did you know Shel was going with Madeline at the time you were seeing him?" Cohen asked.

"I knew about her. He'd mention her sometimes, like about things they had done together. I knew he stayed over there a lot. It was like he was playing house."

"What do you mean, 'playing house'?"

"Oh, she has kids, a boy and a girl. And they went on family outings—picnics, beach, that kinda stuff. And he used to play baseball with her son. He'd tell me about it."

"Tell us exactly what happened when Madeline found out you were seeing Shel," Cohen ordered in a gentle but firm voice.

Chicky began without hesitation. "One afternoon Shel and I were sitting in the backyard at my place and I heard my doorbell ring. So I yelled out, 'Come on 'round back.' I thought it was some friend of mine or someone for one of my roommates. But it was her."

"Madeline Jennings-Ellison."

"Yeah. Madeline whatever."

"And when was this?" Cohen asked.

"Let's see. It was right when summer school ended. Right before I went home. My parents wanted me to go to Hampton Bays with them for a couple of weeks before fall semester.

And I did, around the middle of August. So it was right before that."

"So, the middle of August, you and Shel were sitting in your backyard and Madeline rang your bell and then came around back," Cohen summed up.

Chicky continued, "She was furious. She came right up to us and she screamed, 'So it's true, it's true,' and she was crying and Shel kept saying, 'Calm down, calm down.' And that just started her up more. She started calling him names—liar and bastard and cheat—and he just kept trying to calm her down. And finally she said that Lou Hammer had told her he was seeing me."

"You mean Professor Hammer? He told Madeline about Shel and you?"

Chicky nodded.

"And before Professor Hammer told her, Madeline didn't know about you?"

Chicky said, "I guess she thought he wasn't seeing anyone but her. She was so mad. And she kept saying, 'A sophomore, for God's sake. Just look at her,' as if it was ridiculous, as if I was ridiculous. But Shel just said very calmly, 'Madeline, you knew I saw other women. I told you—we both agreed—our relationship was good the way it was. We didn't need possessiveness.' And she just kept screaming. And he said they should talk about it later when she'd calmed down and they were alone. There were people looking out of windows of houses on both sides to see what all the commotion was about. But Madeline said, 'No. There'll be no later. This is it.' Then she pointed at me and said, 'Take her. She's what you deserve,' like an actress on a soap. And I would've laughed if I hadn't been so mad. Then she stomped off."

"And that was the end of it?"

"Hah! More like the beginning. She changed her mind pretty fast about not seeing him again. She began to call him day and night. She called at his apartment and shrieked at him. She called my place and when I answered the phone she'd scream 'Bitch' at me. I had to take my phone off the hook many a night. Shel told her she was a nut and they were through. He threatened her that if she called anymore he'd tell the police and have her arrested for disturbing the peace."

"Did that stop her?"

"Well, she stopped. Not right away. But it's been months now since I've heard from her. And I don't think Shel has either . . ." Abruptly Chicky stopped talking, stared at Cohen.

Then, breathlessly, she asked, "Wow. D'you think . . . it was Madeline killed him?"

Cohen didn't answer. He tipped forward in his chair suddenly and asked, "Do you have any idea, or did Shel ever say why Professor Hammer told Madeline about you?"

Chicky thought hard. "Shel said something about Lou Hammer being an unstable character, about his being jealous of him. Maybe that's why."

"Thank you for your help, Chicky," Cohen said. "That's probably all we need, but we may have to call on you again." He stood up.

Chicky got up also, a sad look on her face. "Well, I'd be glad to help you get whoever killed Shel. He meant a lot to me." With a sad little smile at Hughes, which he gallantly returned, Chicky Manning left the room silently on her New Balance running shoes.

When Hughes had closed the door behind her, Cohen shook his head and said, "He meant a lot to her. Whatever happened to boy-girl relationships, ya know, one boy with one girl. Are all the young people like them today?"

"Whaddya mean, young?" Hughes said. "Silverman was pushing forty."

"That's true," Cohen said thoughtfully. "But he was one of those sixties relics. I mean the young people your age. How old're you?"

"Twenty-seven," Hughes replied. "Maybe on the college campuses some girls are like Chicky. Not U. Mass Boston night school. Or South Boston, where I come from. Around there a girl like Chicky would get herself a good paddling on the backside."

"So Hammer tried to mess up Silverman's arrangements," Cohen said thoughtfully. "And Madeline did not want to end it as she told us she did this morning."

Hughes picked it up. "Hammer set her up. She had reason to be pretty angry with both of them, didn't she?"

"Find Madeline Jennings-Ellison. Get her in here again as soon as possible, even if it means moving some of the others around. Who have we got next?"

Madeline Jennings-Ellison sat on the edge of the chair next to Cohen's desk. Her large green eyes were anxious. Her fingers kneaded the strap of her floppy leather shoulder bag. Her faded jeans seemed molded to her body. She was a very pretty woman, Cohen thought. Looked much younger than her thirty-six years. In fact, dressed the way she was, she reminded him of Rachel and Becca, his two teenage daughters. And she acted like them, too. As if she knew all about it already—whatever it was.

"But I told you everything I could this morning," she was insisting in a voice that fell short of its usual authority.

Cohen came right to the point. "You didn't tell us it was

Professor Hammer who told you that Professor Silverman was 'seeing' . . ."—Cohen hesitated on the word for only a second—". . . that he was seeing Chicky Manning."

Madeline seemed genuinely puzzled. "That didn't seem important."

"When we talked this morning, you also downplayed the importance of your discovery of Professor Silverman's relationship with Ms. Manning. In fact, you were very angry when you learned of the relationship between them—angry at both Professor Silverman and Ms. Manning."

"You've been talking to Chicky Manning," Madeline said angrily.

Cohen didn't deny it.

"Wait a minute," Madeline exploded, leaning toward Cohen, pointing a finger at him. "You trying to say *I* had reason to kill Shel?"

"I'm trying to say that the explanation you gave this morning of your relationship with Professor Silverman was less than open."

"I've told only the truth," Madeline said, trying for but not quite achieving her self-confident air.

"For example," Cohen continued, ignoring her remark, "you might have told us that Professor Hammer was the one who told you Professor Silverman was seeing Chicky Manning. I would've been interested to know why he did that."

"You would've been?" Her question was a mixture of curiosity and disbelief. "Well, as I told you, I can answer that, only I didn't think it was important. See, Lou Hammer wants everything Shel has. I think he'd like to *be* Shel if he could . . ." She caught herself and gave an ironic laugh, "not dead, of course. But Lou is kinda weird. Their relationship is weird—was. I could have sworn Shel hated him, yet he did so much for him. And I've seen that look in Lou's shiny black snake's eyes when Shel is—was—lecturing. Shel had brains and style. Lou has neither. When Shel and I were happy together—laughing, whispering, holding hands—there were times I'd see Lou watching us, as if . . . as if he were trying to memorize Shel or something." She laughed again, this time with a touch of embarrassment. "Y'know, sometimes I thought he was in love with Shel."

"In love with him?" Cohen asked, using his best nondirective approach.

"Well—yeah—like in gay."

"Uh-huh," Cohen said noncommittally.

"But he isn't," she said definitely. "Gay, I mean."

"He isn't?"

"You see, I was the one he was after."

"Oh?"

"I guess because anything Shel was doing looked so desirable to him. I was in his office the day he told me about Shel and Chicky Manning. He'd asked me if I would be the student representative on the faculty lecture committee, and I said I would even though he was a Class A jerk. I thought it might be fun to help pick speakers, introduce them, drum up student support. So I was in his office that day going over a list of possible speakers and, all of a sudden, before I even knew what was happening, he grabbed me and kissed me, this big, wet, passionate kiss—not the kind of kiss you can fake. I could feel the heat. It was sickening. I pushed him away and said, 'Hey, I'm your best friend's girlfriend.'

"And he said, 'You are making a big mistake. He is fooling around with someone else.'

"And I got really mad, told him he was a liar. That's when

he told me about that little adolescent twerp Shel was seeing, Chicky Manning. And I ran out of there right in the middle of his spiel about how he was in love with me and did nothing but dream about me and how happy he could make me and shit—I mean stuff—like that. I left him there with his tongue hanging out, the ugly jerk . . ." she trailed off.

"And then?" Cohen prodded.

Madeline's eyes narrowed, suddenly aware of the intensity with which Cohen was listening. Her eyes flicked over to Hughes, who was watching her also. He looked down at his notebook quickly. She knew they were waiting for something and she stopped talking, squirmed in her chair.

Cohen said, "This morning you told us that you were the one who broke off the relationship with Professor Silverman because you, in your own words, 'realized he was a phony.' Since then we've heard that it was Professor Silverman who wanted to end it."

"Chicky Manning," Madeline said bitterly.

Cohen waited, said nothing.

"It was all Lou Hammer's fault. If he hadn't told me the way he did . . . It got me so mad . . . I marched right over to Chicky's place. And there he was mooning over that stupid kid. I told him I never wanted to see him again. Then by the time I cooled off, he blew *me* away."

Madeline's face was in her hands, her body shaking with sobs. "I wanted him back. I lost him. All because of that asshole Hammer. And now he's dead."

Over her bowed head, Cohen and Hughes exchanged appraising looks.

CHAPTER 14

Thursday Morning, April 26, 1984

Cohen and Hughes sat at their usual places. Laid out on the desk in front of them were several new reports.

"So it checks out," Cohen said briskly. He tapped a typed sheet with his fingertips. "Hammer was killed with the same gun that killed Silverman, shot at close range in the right temple, the gun firmly clasped in his right hand. A twenty-two English service revolver, the kind soldiers brought back as souvenirs by the truckload after World War Two. So no chance of tracing it.

"Hammer's wounds and his position were consistent with a self-inflicted act. Time of death estimated at early yesterday morning, sometime between three and five A.M. No fingerprints except Hammer's found on the gun or anywhere in the apartment. And no fingerprints except Hammer's on the note. You say that your canvass of Hammer's apartment building and the nearby buildings gave us nothing?"

Hughes shook his head. "Nothing. Nobody saw anyone near Hammer's apartment Tuesday night or early Wednesday morning. There are still a couple of people we haven't been able to talk to yet. One lady in the hospital having a baby and a guy who went on vacation yesterday morning."

Cohen tapped with his pencil. "So we got nobody saw anything at Hammer's place. And we got no fingerprints other than his. And we got a suicide note signed by the victim with his fingerprints and his signature, which the handwriting experts in Boston tested against other samples of Hammer's signature. Definitely his. Oh yeah, we also got the pen he wrote it with on the desk beside the note, with only his prints on the pen, too. And, to top it off, we got his prints on the typewriter keys. They were able to lift some good ones. Nobody else's but Hammer's on the keys. If someone else typed the note and wiped off the keys, he would've wiped off Hammer's prints as well as his own. And if someone typed with gloves on, he would've blurred Hammer's prints." He waved the suicide note. "Letter keys had multiple prints on them blurred by contact, but not wiped off." Cohen looked at Hughes for his reaction to all this information.

Hughes didn't hesitate for a moment. "Could have typed the note and signed it under duress," Hughes said.

Cohen smiled. "Yeah. Happens," he said.

Encouraged, Hughes went on. "Somebody could've come in there with a gun, held it to his head, made him type the note and sign it, then shot him in the head."

Cohen was shaking his head. "Happens. But not this time."

"Why not?"

"Look at how this note is typed. Perfect. Not a mistake on it. Typed firmly, evenly, by someone very cool, someone who didn't have a gun at his head, looks like to me. Hammer's typewriter is one of those little Smith-Corona portables, not electric, the kind where if you hesitate over a letter, if you bang one key harder than another, if your hand is shaking, shows right up in the typing. Anyway, the experts compared this note against other samples of Hammer's typing. He used the hunt-and-peck system, both pointer fingers. This note was typed the same way."

"Okay," Hughes began, scrutinizing the note again. "But it's still possible he typed it under duress."

"I'm not saying it's not possible," Cohen said. He handed Hughes a sheet of paper. "Here's the report just came in from the research department in Boston. I think you'll find it interesting."

Hughes read aloud, "Professor Sheldon S. Silverman was a graduate student at Page University in Sylvana, New York, when the science center was bombed by student activists on May 1, 1968. He was named as a coconspirator by Daniel Connors, a suspect in the bombing murders. But since no connection could be proven between Silverman and Connors, Silverman was not indicted by the grand jury. Silverman's plea of innocence was supported by the testimony of graduate student Louis J. Hammer that Silverman was working with him throughout the evening of May 1, 1968. Two men were killed in the bombing, a graduate student, James Lincoln Kent, and the university night watchman, Harry McVey. Connors, also a graduate student, was convicted of murder and was sentenced to twenty-five years at the Attica Correctional Facility."

Cohen listened to Hughes read the material. The suicide note still bothered him even though the experts had found nothing bogus about it. When Hughes had finished reading the report, Cohen read the note again while Hughes looked on: "I shot Professor Sheldon Silverman, and I now shall do the same for myself. In my judgement Silverman deserved to die. He was the murderer of three. I have protected him all these years, but I can no longer endure the empty lie my life has become."

Hughes said, "Hammer was covering Silverman and just couldn't stand it anymore."

Cohen said, "You saw Silverman's body. Do you really think someone who was just plain fed up could have done a job like that?"

"He was shot up real bad," Hughes said.

"Right. Sure seems like whoever killed him hated the guy."

"Well, Hammer might've hated him . . ." Hughes began.

"More likely Silverman hated Hammer," Cohen interrupted. "It was Hammer who had power over Silverman and Hammer who messed up a good thing he had going with Madeline."

Hughes sat still, at a loss.

Cohen jabbed at the note with a finger. "What about this 'murderer of three'?" he asked. "Say Hammer knew Silverman was somehow responsible for the deaths of Kent and McVey. Who's the third?"

Hughes rubbed his chin. "Good question," he said.

They sat silently, Cohen looking out the window, Hughes reading the suicide note yet again.

"That guy who took the rap . . ." Cohen checked the note again. ". . . Daniel Connors. Call the FBI and Albany. Make sure the facts we got are accurate. Find out if he's still in Attica. Sometimes these guys get out early. Also do a rundown on both victims, Kent and McVey, and their families."

Dutifully, Hughes jotted down these new tasks in his notebook.

"Strange," Cohen said, tapping his pencil, looking beyond Hughes into his clattering air conditioner that rocked on the window sill, "that no one seemed to think Hammer had much ability, yet Silverman was a genius."

"By his own admission," Hughes added.

"Yes," Cohen agreed. "I gather he would have been the first to say so. But he was considered very bright and he was awarded that special chair."

"And Hammer wasn't considered to be so smart."

"You thinking what I'm thinking?" Cohen asked.

"What's that?"

"They struck a deal. Hammer gives Silverman the alibi. Silverman shares his brains with Hammer. Maybe even wrote that book on Wallace Stevens for him so he could get tenure."

"Yeah," Hughes said with admiration. "Yeah."

"But why does Hammer kill Silverman now? After all these years? Just when he's coming up for tenure? Just when his 'protection' of Silverman might really pay off?"

"Something to do with that appointment Silverman got?" Hughes suggested.

"The Finstermann Chair. Recognition of exceptional merit. The high point in a man's career. Maybe that set Hammer off. Maybe Hammer was beginning to think he wasn't going to get tenure. So Silverman's appointment may have made him mad, real mad, at Silverman, who either couldn't or wouldn't do whatever was necessary to get him tenure. That's probably what they argued about. At any rate, that's what Silverman told Froming right before he was killed."

Hughes said thoughtfully, "But the note doesn't sound angry, like Hammer would be after a big argument."

"Good point," Cohen said, so genuinely that Hughes

flushed with pleasure. "The writer of the note sounds con-science-stricken, not angry. Silverman deserves to die and I've been living an empty lie."

"You're a poet."

"Aw, shucks," Cohen said, but he was thinking hard and Hughes knew enough not to interrupt him. He said finally, "So, we got two separate motives or maybe a combination of motives. One: anger. Hammer blows him away because he isn't coming through. And, two: crisis of conscience. Hammer kills him because he's fed up with protecting a murderer. An excess of motives. Who needs it?"

Cohen sat up straight and stacked the reports into a neat pile. He was beginning to get a feel for this case. He said to Hughes, "You've got a couple of hours before our afternoon interviews. Find out everything about what happened at Page University on May 1, 1968. I want bios on all the people involved. Get all the police and FBI reports, newspaper stories, anything you can."

Hughes got up to leave, but turned at the door. "You still think it's possible someone could have murdered both of them and made it look like murder-suicide?"

Cohen smiled. Hughes would never let him forget the obvious, even for a moment. He could almost see Hughes's sluggish mind grinding away like an old-fashioned adding machine. "I still think it's possible," he said, and he began to study the reports on his desk.

CHAPTER 15

Thursday Afternoon, April 26, 1984

Lisa Davis paced her box of a living room. She stopped every once in a while to stare out the window at the Charles River below, dappled and gray in a fine April rain that hovered like misty curtains around her windows. Ever since her interview with Lieutenant Cohen yesterday morning, something had been bothering her, something about one of her students, a frail, sad girl named Dove Kent. She couldn't get her out of her mind.

She picked up the afternoon edition of *The Boston Globe* from the coffee table. The headlines screamed at her: MURDER-SUICIDE AT ADDISON. She glanced quickly at Silverman's smiling face and at the serious, ugly face of Hammer beside it on the front page and threw the paper back on the table. Standing at her window, she looked out at the buildings of Cambridge beyond the river. On a clear day she could see the Boston skyscrapers, sticking up like pencils on the horizon. Not today. Lisa sighed and took another turn around the room. Then she stood at the window again and looked down beneath her dripping balcony to Greenough Boulevard, where cars flashed by on the shimmery black asphalt.

Finally, she marched over to the kitchenette and picked up the receiver of the white wall phone over the counter. She punched the buttons and frowned as she waited and tightened the cord around her index finger.

After three rings a woman's voice answered, "*Boston Globe* News Department."

Lisa held her breath for a moment and then let it out explosively. "Brad Newman, please," she said, feeling indecisive again. Well, maybe he wouldn't even be there. Maybe he didn't even work there anymore. She hadn't talked to him in almost eight months. She twisted the phone cord around her finger one more time.

"Brad Newman." The sound of his voice, aggressive, boyish, made her heart start to thud.

"Brad, it's Lisa. Lisa Davis."

There was a pause. Then he shouted, his voice vibrating in her ear. "Lisa, God, Lisa. How are you?"

"I'm fine. I've been working hard. You know I'm at Addison. But it's been good, really good. Just what I needed." She was aware of rushing her words, saying too much. She stopped.

"Great," he said. "I'm glad it's going well."

"And how are you?" She pictured him as he must look right now. Tie loosened. Dark hair falling into his eyes above his large, sharp nose.

"Fine. Well, okay, anyway. I tried to get the Addison story, but it went to Graves," he said bitterly.

Brad and Graves were always competing. "Too bad," Lisa replied, instantly on his side, just as she used to be.

"But of course I've been following it anyway. You must have known Silverman and Hammer. I was going to call you if I got the story."

"That's what I'm calling about, the Addison case," Lisa said with relief at the chance to explain. "I've got what may be a lead, but I want to check it out before I go to the police."

Brad laughed, that deep laugh that she had loved at first and then grown to distrust. "That's my girl," he said, "always right there when the bodies start to fall."

"It's not my fault," she said in mock anger, aware that they were sliding back into the old teasing patterns. "Not my fault that people seem to get murdered around me. I have nothing to do with it. I *did* find the body, though, the first one, Professor Silverman."

"That must have been awful," Brad said soberly, "with five bullets in him."

"It was awful."

"Maybe you should stay out of this. The police know what they're doing."

"It's not the same as the O'Neil murder," Lisa said. "I know I went a little too far then, took unnecessary chances. This time I just want to check out my hunch before I take it to the police. And if it turns out I'm wrong, I'll drop it and go about my business. God knows, I've got enough to do, taking two courses, being T.A. for one of them, and freelancing."

"How is the freelancing going?" Brad asked.

She remembered that he had promised to help. "Pretty well," she answered. "I've been getting articles about Addison into the local papers. Good start for a portfolio, at any rate."

"Great." A pause. Then, "So where do I come in?"

"I'd like to look something up in the *Globe* files," she said quickly. "I know I could probably find it at any library, on microfilm, but I'd like it in a hurry because if I find anything, I want to take it to the police, get it off my mind." She stopped talking, wondering if her reasoning sounded valid to him or if he thought she was just looking for an excuse to see him again.

"That's easily arranged," he said. "When can you come over?"

"How about now?"

"Fine. I'll call Barbara at the library and get it in the works. What do you want?"

"Everything about the explosion at Page University in May of 1968. Today's paper gave only a brief account."

"You got it. And listen, stop by my office first. You remember where it is, don't you?"

"I remember."

As Lisa drove east toward Boston on the Mass Turnpike, she thought about Dove Kent. Dove was a student in her section, one of a group of twelve students who met Tuesdays and Thursdays at four o'clock in the small seminar room next to the English office to sigh and fidget through discussions of one another's papers and the larger themes of American Journalism as presented in the morning lectures by Professor Silverman, the late Professor Silverman.

She had noticed Dove right away. A nonfidgeter. In her eyes the peaceful expression of the dead. On the first day of class Lisa asked her students to write about an event in their lives that had made a lasting impression. That evening, red-penciling her way through papers with titles like "A Turning Point in My Life: Making Cheerleader," and "My Job at Florsheim Shoes and How It Changed Me," she came to Dove's paper, "My Mother's Suicide."

Her pencil fell to the floor, unnoticed, as she read of the

day, six years before, when Dove, age twelve, had broken the lock on her mother's bedroom door with a hammer and tried to save her mother's life by tying handkerchiefs around her bleeding wrists. Despite her efforts, Mrs. Kent was dead by the time the ambulance crew arrived twenty minutes later. She had used Dove's razor to do the job, a fact that troubled the girl greatly.

After reading the concluding sentence, "This event made a lasting impression on me," Lisa sat very still for a long time. Then she picked up her red pencil and wrote gently in the upper right-hand corner of the first page, "Please see me after class."

Dove Kent's real name was Little Dove Kent, but she had dropped the "Little" and called herself simply Dove or, as on the school records, L. Dove Kent. She told Lisa that when she was born, in 1965, her parents wanted to commemorate their Indian brothers and sisters who had been so poorly treated by the white man, so they named their first and only child Little Dove. Dove's father had died when she was very young, and her mother, "basically a very impractical person," had supported herself and her young daughter by typing and babysitting when she could get work at all. Since her mother's death, Dove had lived in Pittsburgh with her mother's sister, who was in and out of mental institutions. "Really a very spaced-out person." Dove had brought up her two cousins, had trained them to be self-sufficient, planning for the day when she would go off to college.

"Why did you choose Addison?" Lisa had asked, thinking how far away from the two needy cousins it was.

Instead of responding, Dove's face had grown secret and strange, her eyes dull, her mouth closed tight, like a door shutting in Lisa's face.

Since that first talk with the girl, Lisa had become increasingly aware of Dove's peculiarities. She could sit through an entire class with her small raisin-dark eyes staring and empty. She never seemed to talk to any of the other students. When called to Lisa's office to discuss a paper, she would sit with that empty expression on her face except when the conversation turned to political activism. Then her eyes would start to flash, her still face would become animated, suddenly beautiful, as she argued for a nuclear freeze, for stopping aid to El Salvador, for free nationwide abortion clinics.

"When my parents were grad students in the late sixties," Dove would say, "their goal was to make the world a better place. All the kids here think about is the Dow-Jones average or whether their Chem grade is high enough to get them into medical school."

Lisa wondered about those idealistic parents of Dove's— what they were trying to accomplish and how they went about it—but every time she asked about them, Dove would get that faraway look in her eyes.

"What was your father studying?" produced only a tight-lipped "Science."

"Where were your parents at school?" earned her a startled look that seemed to change to anger and the answer, "New York," through clamped lips.

Lisa stopped asking, but she continued to invite Dove into her office because she felt the girl needed a friend. And soon Lisa discovered that there was another subject that could provoke a response in Dove, and that was the subject of Professor Sheldon Silverman. Dove was taking two of his courses, an unusual choice for a freshman, since freshmen were advised to diversify their programs. Dove's interest in Silverman was intense. She was always eager to talk about him, particularly to discuss what he was really like beneath what she thought of as the public posturing of his lectures. She questioned his views on freedom of the press, nuclear disarmament, U.S. involvement in Latin America. She suspected that his hopeful attitude toward Russia and the possibility of negotiations on disarmament was what she called a "phony liberalism."

On Monday afternoon Dove had come into Lisa's office to discuss her latest paper. She seemed paler than usual. As she sat down, she caught sight of Lisa's copy of the *Addison News*, which lay on top of a pile of student papers on the desk. On the front page, beneath the headline SILVERMAN NAMED TO FINSTERMANN CHAIR, the photograph of Silverman beamed. Dove stared at it.

Lisa handed the paper to her. "Have you seen it?" she asked.

Dove did not put out a hand to take it, and Lisa let the newspaper fall back onto the pile of papers.

"Talk about fame and fortune," Lisa said lightly.

She was surprised to see Dove's pale face flood with color, red blotches the size of geraniums blossoming on her cheeks. "That bastard, that bloodsucking bastard!" Dove exclaimed.

She hates him, Lisa realized for the first time. She's obsessed with him because she hates him. "Why do you hate him?" she asked.

The color left Dove's face. She slumped into her chair and rested her face in her hands.

"Are you all right?" Lisa asked, touching the girl's thin shoulder. "What is it? What's the matter?"

"I know some things about him," Dove began and then stopped.

"What? What do you know?" Lisa asked.

"I know he's a hypocrite and places no value on human lives," Dove said, but despite Lisa's repeated questions, she couldn't get any more out of the girl.

Now as Lisa drove toward Boston, she kept thinking that Silverman had been murdered only a few hours after that conversation with Dove. She worried that Dove was somehow involved in his death. Yesterday morning, when Lieutenant Cohen asked her if she knew if Silverman had any enemies, she had thought of Dove, but she hadn't mentioned her. Now she was really worried that Dove had been his enemy.

Lisa had read today's *Globe* article about the murder carefully. The police speculated that Hammer had given Silverman the alibi that kept him from being implicated in the 1968 bombing of a science building at Page University in which two men were killed. They also believed that Hammer had been blackmailing Silverman all these years so that he could keep his academic appointment at Addison. The two men had an argument in Silverman's office Monday afternoon, and an hour or so later, Silverman was murdered brutally, shot several times before he was finished off with a bullet to the heart. The police believed that Hammer had murdered Silverman and then taken his own life early yesterday morning, on the day that he was supposed to report to the Braeton police for questioning.

It made sense, Lisa thought, as she turned onto the Southeast Expressway, often called the Southeast Distressway, and headed for Morrissey Boulevard. It made sense, all right, but she kept seeing Dove's face, mottled with anger, and she kept hearing Dove's voice, full of hatred for Silverman. There had been something between Dove and Silverman that made her hate him, and Lisa had to find out what it was.

CHAPTER 16

When she stepped into Brad's cluttered little office, he jumped up and came toward her. He put his arms around her and kissed her cheek. Then he held her away to look at her. "It's good to see you," he said.

Embarrassed, she repeated his words in a more serious tone than she'd intended. "It's good to see you."

"Here. Sit down. Let's talk for a minute. Then we'll go down to the library. Barbara's getting what you want." He scooped up a mound of papers from a chair and pulled it near the desk.

Lisa sat down, suddenly self-conscious. She crossed her legs. She'd lost some weight recently and she took courage from knowing her legs looked lean in the slim jeans and high boots. She wore a black sleeveless sweater. Her dark hair was as frizzy and unruly as always. She patted it down anxiously.

It wasn't until she was sitting there that she began to realize exactly what she had done. With Brad's big ego, her call must have seemed like a signal that she wanted to start up with him again. Did she? She'd been seeing Sam for three months now, trying to be in love with him. Maybe this visit was just a test she'd devised for herself, to see if the feelings for Brad were still there.

"You look great," he was saying. "I'm glad things are going well at Addison."

"It's surprising to me how much I like the studying and the teaching." She looked at him, his strong features, his friendly smile. "I'm glad you're fine."

"Oh, yes." He nodded. "Fine. Fine."

There was a long silence.

"You look great," he repeated. "You don't know how many times since last September, since you told me how impossible I was, I thought of calling you."

Lisa's eyebrows shot up in disbelief.

"I thought about it. But then I said to myself, You're just as impossible as when she told you off, so why call?"

"There's a certain logic in that," she said. "So why did you want to?"

"Want to what?"

"Want to call. Why did you want to call?"

He moved a stack of papers from his desk onto the window ledge. He looked at her, flashing the old cocky smile. "Because you're some dish, that's why."

"Right," she said calmly. "You're just as impossible as when I told you off."

"I wanted to call you because I missed you, goddammit. Don't you think I've got any feelings?"

"I wasn't sure," Lisa answered seriously. She remembered that it had taken her a long time to figure out the pattern of his behavior: his hot pursuit of her until he thought he'd won her, then his indifference until she gave up on him, which started the pursuit again. That kind of game might be all right for kids, but she was almost thirty-one years old, ready for something more substantial than a hide-and-seek relationship. She'd put up with it for a long time—too long—because she thought she was in love with him. He made her feel alive, excited. With him she was often angry and frustrated, but never bored, which was more than she could say for most of the men she had dated before and since.

Finally, right before she started Addison last fall, she told him that she couldn't continue seeing him, that his unreliability made her miserable. Afterward she kept hoping he'd call, tell her he was ready to be with her and her alone. The call never came.

"I didn't call because I didn't want to give you the chance to bite my head off again."

So that's the way he saw it, her finally telling him how she felt. It hadn't been easy, with him wisecracking through her whole speech. "That wasn't biting your head off," she said. "That was called leveling with you."

"Well, okay, you did that. You leveled with me. Told me I was ruining your life, that I was unreliable, incapable of real love." He ran a hand through his dark, straight hair, gave his head a shake as if he were sincerely baffled.

He hadn't understood any of it. Still didn't. She wasn't surprised.

"Anyway, I did miss you. And I'm glad everything's okay with you," he said.

"And I'm glad you're okay, too," she said, meaning it.

"And," he began, paused, then began again, "and I've found someone to put up with me. I've been seeing my old high school girlfriend. June Gold. She's the one I told you about. Married Danny Finkle. Worked as a secretary to put him through med school. Then he dumped her for some nurse."

Why did the news of his old/new girlfriend June hit her like a punch to the rib cage? "Great," she said. "That's great."

"How about you?" he asked. "You found that perfect man yet?"

Lisa shrugged, trying to hide her feelings. "Perfect? You taught me there was no such thing," she said with what she hoped was a sophisticated toss of her wild curls.

Brad threw his head back and laughed, showing his mouthful of large, even teeth in a way that Lisa remembered only too well. He looked at her with a flicker of that old flirtatious expression. "Same old Lisa," he said with genuine appreciation.

"But," Lisa continued, "I have been seeing someone. Someone who's really good for me," she finished pointedly. That, at least, was true.

"Wonderful," Brad said with a little too much enthusiasm. "You deserve it."

They took the elevator downstairs to the newspaper library where Brad introduced her to Barbara Gray, who was in charge of the files.

"I'll leave you here to work," Brad said. "Just ask Barbara for anything you need. I'll be at my desk. Buzz me at 116 if anything comes up."

Lisa opened the first canister of microfilm dated Friday, May 3, 1968, and rolled the film into the viewing machine. The story was on the front page, next to an article on the demonstrations and student takeovers at Columbia University. The headline read: TWO KILLED ON N.Y. CAMPUS. Dateline: May 2, Sylvana N.Y. Lisa read:

> Two men were killed in a bomb explosion at the Lohr Science Center at Page University: Harry McVey, sixty-two, a watchman, and James Lincoln Kent, twenty-nine, a graduate student. A third man,

Daniel Connors, twenty-four, also a graduate student, was injured in the explosion, and is being held by the police for questioning. Damages are estimated in excess of $400,000.

Lisa stared at the printed name that leaped out at her—James Lincoln Kent. Twenty-nine years old when he died in 1968, old enough to have a baby daughter two years old then, a daughter who would be eighteen years old now and who could be a freshman at Addison. If Dove were the daughter of the man killed in the explosion in 1968, was it a coincidence that she was now a freshman at the same college at which Sheldon Silverman, who was somehow involved in that bombing, was an associate professor? Lisa shook her head. No. No coincidence. She thought of Dove's intense interest in Silverman, her obsession with the difference between what he said and what he believed. She thought of Dove's calling him a bastard in her office on the day his appointment to the coveted Finstermann Chair was announced, the day of his death.

Brow furrowed in concentration, she bent over the viewer, rereading the article. If Dove's father was one of the men who was killed in the bombing, did Dove believe that Silverman was responsible for his death and—a new thought—even for her mother's death nine years later? Had Dove killed Silverman, making him suffer first, to pay for whatever he had done? But why had she waited so long? Well, she'd been growing up. The obsession with Silverman, the need for revenge, could have been growing inside her. And why had she killed Hammer as well? Because Hammer had protected Silverman, kept him from being charged with murder by providing him with an alibi. Far-fetched? Lisa tapped her pencil on the edge of the desk. Far-fetched. But possible. If James Lincoln Kent had had a child. If that child were Little Dove Kent. Possible.

The telephone at her desk buzzed. "How ya doing?" Brad asked.

"I think I've found something. One of the men who was killed in that explosion at Page in 1968 was a James Lincoln Kent. Could be Dove Kent's father. She said he died when she was two."

"I'll be right down."

Lisa put another article into the viewer. GRADUATE STU-DENT CLEARED IN PAGE BOMB MURDERS, she read.

A grand jury today found insufficient evidence to indict graduate student Sheldon S. Silverman in the bombing at Page University on May 2 despite the testimony of Daniel Connors, who is being held on suspicion of murder. Connors claimed that while he and James Kent placed the bomb in the laboratory, Silverman was posted in front of the building to prevent anyone from entering. Connors stated that because Silverman left his post, the night watchman, Harry McVey, entered the building and tried to stop Connors and Kent. In the struggle the bomb exploded, killing Kent and McVey. The grand jury found no evidence linking Silverman to the crime. The testimony of graduate student Louis Jason Hammer that he was with Silverman during the night of May 1/2 helped confirm Silverman's story.

Brad came into the library and read the story. Then they put an October 1968 paper in the viewer. Together they looked at the photograph of a thin waiflike young woman wearing jeans and a leather jacket, her long pale hair hanging almost to her waist. In her arms a child with the same pale hair stared wide-eyed into the camera.

Brad read the caption aloud: "Stella Kent holding her

daughter, Little Dove, at the trial of Daniel Connors for murder in the bombing at Page University, Sylvana, N.Y. Mrs. Kent's husband, James Lincoln Kent, was one of two men killed in the bombing. Connors was convicted as charged and sentenced to twenty-five years in prison."

Lisa couldn't take her eyes off the photograph. "Oh, my God," she breathed.

"Your student?" Brad asked.

Lisa nodded.

Brad studied the picture. "Lookalikes, aren't they?"

Lisa rolled the film out of the viewer. "So much so that it's scary."

"Why scary?" Brad asked.

"Dove's mother was unstable. She committed suicide when Dove was twelve. It frightens me to think how unstable Dove may be, especially when I think of how she must have blamed Silverman for her father's death."

"You think she killed Silverman?"

"I think it's possible. If it's true that Silverman was supposed to keep anyone from entering the building where her father was setting a bomb, and he didn't, then I suppose he was responsible for Kent's death. If it's true."

Brad said, "Maybe Silverman didn't have anything to do with that bombing—as he insisted—but whoever killed him and Hammer figured the police would believe he did and, therefore, accept the murder-suicide theory."

"Possible."

Brad looked at the photograph of Dove and her mother again. "It seems crazy to me that grown-up men would do that—set a bomb off like that in a school building, for Chrissake," Brad said.

"They were kinda crazy in the late sixties, those who

wanted to blow things up to improve society. Like Jane Alpert. I just read her autobiography. But they believed in what they were doing, anyway."

"Not our late professor, maybe."

"Not if it's true that he ran out as soon as there was trouble," Lisa said. "And I think Dove believes that's just what he did. On Monday, the day he was killed, she told me he was a hypocrite who put no value on human lives."

"Connors had reason to hate Silverman, too. He was convicted of murder," Brad said thoughtfully. "How long did they give him?"

Lisa looked into the viewer again and said, "Twenty-five years."

"What if, somehow, he's out. Maybe he came back and killed them both for setting him up that way."

Lisa nodded. "I thought about him, too." She looked at the boxes of film on the desk without really seeing them. "She's only a child and she's been through so much. She found her mother after her mother had cut her wrists. She tried to save her."

"That's awful," Brad said with feeling. "But do you really think she could've murdered them?"

"She's a strange, troubled child. Truthfully, I don't know what she's capable of."

Brad took his little black notebook out of his shirt pocket. "Let's go over the possibilities," he suggested.

She watched him write POSSIBILITIES in bold block letters at the top of a page. Sitting so close to him, watching his square hands, she felt attracted to him again. What was the matter with her? Was she forgetting how his lack of commitment had nearly driven her crazy? He hurt me, she reminded herself. And if I gave him the chance, he'd hurt me again.

He was looking at her expectantly.

"What?" she asked.

"I said, the police seem to buy the murder-suicide explanation."

"They seem to," she said. "It is plausible."

Lisa watched Brad write "1—*MURDER-SUICIDE*" in his firm printing. Under the "1" he wrote "2" just as firmly and said, "Okay, who's two? Your Little Dove?"

Lisa said, "I can see her hating Silverman. But why Hammer?"

"Why not? Hammer saved Silverman."

"But if her motive was revenge, Hammer had nothing to do with her father's death. James Kent was already dead before Hammer came into the picture."

"Yes, but if it hadn't been for Hammer, Silverman would've been punished as he deserved to be. Anyway, who says she's completely rational?" Brad asked.

"Good point," Lisa conceded. She looked at the photograph in the viewer again. Little Dove Kent sat on her mother's hip and clung to the long hair with her tiny fingers, like a monkey. Lisa sighed and rolled the film out of the machine. "Do you think I should go to the police with this?" she asked as she put the film back into the canister.

"Of course," Brad said. "Anyway, they probably know about it."

Lisa sighed. "She is such a strange girl, Brad. I'm the only one she talks to. Although she is beginning to warm up to my friend Mary Reardon who is a visiting professor this year and has taken a real interest in her. Other than Mary and me, I've never seen her even talk to anyone."

"You're not doing her any favor by concealing her connection with Silverman. If she didn't do it, she'll be cleared."

Lisa said nothing. She hoped his confidence in the law was well founded.

Lisa watched as Brad wrote, "3—*Connors*" and put a question mark after his name.

"I'll see what I can find out about Connors," Brad said. "Also, we should find out about any surviving relatives of Mc-Vey and of Kent, other than Dove."

Lisa agreed.

"Anyone at Addison who was at Page in 1968?" Brad asked.

"Not that I know of," Lisa said. "But there is a graduate student, Madeline Jennings-Ellison, who was going with Silverman last year. Then he dumped her, or so rumor has it. Maybe she killed him. But that wouldn't explain Hammer's death." As she talked, Lisa gathered her papers and notebooks into her briefcase. She stood up and said, "Thanks, Brad. I appreciate your help. Now that I know about Dove's father, I'm not happy about it. I like that murder-suicide scenario."

Brad smiled. "Well, relax. That's probably just what it was. Just tell Lieutenant Cohen. He'll take it from there. He's a good man. I've watched him conduct several cases over the past couple of years."

Lisa started to leave, but he stopped her with a hand on her shoulder. His touch sent electric currents down her arm. "By the way," he said. "June is having some people over tonight. Just informal, after dinner. Would you come?"

Lisa hesitated and finally stammered, "I have a date. With my friend Sam."

"So much the better," Brad said. "Bring him along."

Lisa hesitated. "I don't know," she said finally. "I'll ask him."

"Come if you can. Twenty-one Stanifore Street. South

End. Right behind the Prudential Building. Off Columbus Avenue."

He accompanied her to the outer door. His invitation had made her uneasy. Apparently, he didn't have lingering feelings about her as she had about him, or he wouldn't have invited her, would he? She found herself torn between wanting to see him as soon as possible and wanting never to see him again.

As she got into her old blue VW in the parking lot, she glanced toward the door and he was standing there, watching her. Damn, she thought, banging her fist on the steering wheel. If Sam were sexier. If Sam were more exciting. Maybe then she wouldn't be having these feelings about Brad. But Sam was Sam. Sweet. Dependable. Solid. Always there. As she drove by the front of the building Brad was no longer in the doorway.

CHAPTER 17

The drive back to Addison from Boston was painfully slow. Lisa hadn't counted on the late afternoon pile-up on the Mass Turnpike. She didn't get to the seminar room until four-fifteen.

"Sorry," she said to the nine or ten students who lounged in the soft chairs surrounding the round oak table. There were always a few students missing. As long as they weren't the same ones all the time, Lisa thought with resignation as she plunked her books and briefcase on the table. Out of the corner of her eye she noticed that Dove Kent was in her usual place, over by the corner, her head resting against the wall, her feet up on the back of a chair. Lisa pushed her curls off her sweaty forehead and opened her briefcase. The students, for the most part, looked toward her attentively as she withdrew the stack of papers she had worked late into the night to correct.

Lisa took a few moments to catch her breath and to observe Dove while the students looked through their papers. Dove's paper lay in her lap, unnoticed. All the other students were flipping pages, searching for comments and checking their grades. But Dove sat with her eyes half-closed as if nothing that was happening around her could affect her.

With so much on her mind, Lisa did little to direct the discussion this afternoon. And the young people, sensing her lack of control, got off the track almost immediately. They much preferred to discuss relationships, sex, personal experience rather than the logical development of ideas and the careful use of language. Instead of guiding the group in an examination of the appalling lack of structure she'd found in these latest papers, Lisa watched Dove. In any other young person, Dove's behavior would have seemed unusual. She sat almost motionless as the students all around her chatted with animation. Most of the time she looked down at her hands or just leaned back against the wall. Lisa hadn't seen her look at her paper once or make any move at all except to raise her head occasionally and look slowly around the room with the dazed, somewhat surprised expression of a person just awakened by a loud noise.

As the students were leaving after class, Lisa decided that she must speak with Dove before going to the police. She watched Dove rise from her seat and begin to glide toward the door, her paper and some notebooks under her arm.

"Dove," Lisa called. "Please stay for a moment. I'd like to talk to you."

Dove turned her whole body toward Lisa, the pale hair swinging over her cheeks like a curtain being drawn. When the others had left, Lisa closed the door. Dove sat down again and looked out the window; she seemed indifferent to Lisa's presence. Lisa had an urgent desire to get a reaction from her somehow. She felt like shaking her. Instead, she began carefully, "I found something out today that disturbed me very much."

Dove turned her face toward Lisa, waiting.

"About you," Lisa continued. "About your father." Still no response from Dove.

"His death," Lisa said and paused.

Dove drew in a huge breath and let it out slowly. "So you know?"

"Yes. I know how he died."

Dove waited still, and Lisa, hesitating, trying to decide how to phrase what she wanted to say, began, "I know how you hated Professor Silverman. Now I see that you must have blamed him for your father's death."

Still no reaction from Dove.

"What I was wondering was how you felt about Silverman's murder."

Suddenly Dove was laughing. It was a horrible sound, low and grating, with no mirth in it. And her eyes were cold and black, like lifeless coals in her white face. Her lips were drawn back, the muscles in her throat working as she laughed. Lisa was horrified at the sound and the sight of her.

Then as suddenly as she had begun, Dove stopped laughing and said in an emotionless, low voice, "How I felt?" Again a bubble of laughter threatened and she waited it out. "I felt happy. Happy that he was dead. That he had suffered."

"How do you know for sure that Silverman was to blame for the explosion that killed your father?" Lisa asked. "He was cleared at the time. He wasn't even tried."

"I know," Dove said firmly. "I just know."

Lisa breathed in deeply. "Then you think he got what he deserved."

"Oh, not what he deserved. Not nearly what he deserved. Hammer was too much of a chicken to give him what he deserved. But at least he got paid back some for what he did."

"So you think Hammer killed Silverman and then himself?" Lisa asked.

Dove's eyes suddenly flashed into life. "Well, of course. Don't you?"

"I don't know. I think it's possible that a third person killed Silverman and then killed Hammer, making it look like murder-suicide. Don't you think that's possible?"

Dove said angrily, "No, I don't think it's possible. Silverman was a murderer. And Hammer covered for him. Hammer lied and cheated and grew to hate the worm he had protected as well as himself. So he killed the worm and then he killed himself. That's what happened. That's what should've happened. And that's what happened." Dove was on her feet, swaying, her voice a hoarse shriek.

Lisa got up and moved toward her, "Dove, I'm sorry . . ." she began.

"No," Dove said in that horrible, expressionless voice. "Don't be sorry. It's a happy ending. Hammer killed him. Murdered the murderer." She was backing away from Lisa toward the door. She opened the door and moved lithely into the corridor.

Lisa called after her, "The police must be told about your past, about your father. They have to know things like that . . ." but she didn't think the girl heard her. Dove was fleeing down the corridor. Her laugh drifted back. Lisa didn't know whether to follow her or not. She was clearly hysterical.

Suddenly drained of energy, Lisa sat back in the chair and waited for her body to stop its violent trembling. At last she was able to stuff her books and the papers of the students who hadn't showed up into her briefcase. On her way out she knocked at Mary's door. No answer. She

glanced at Silverman's locked office door as she headed out
of the building.

Lieutenant Cohen looked steadily at Lisa when she had finished telling him who Little Dove Kent was. Still looking at
her, he leaned way back in his swivel chair, springs creaking
loudly, and continued to gaze at her seriously over the cone of
his fingertips. Suddenly he shot upright with a great protest
of springs, frightening Lisa, who moved to the edge of her
chair. Cohen whipped a crumpled handkerchief from his
pocket and got it to his face just in time to catch the sneeze.

"Excuse me," he said finally, after mopping his nose and
mouth. "Allergies." He blew his nose again and then looked
at Lisa accusingly. "Aren't you the Lisa Davis who helped
solve that murder of the tennis pro over in Cambridge? You
and that *Globe* reporter?"

"That's right."

"I knew your name sounded familiar when I interviewed
you yesterday. Couldn't quite place it. What was his name?"

"Brad Newman."

"Brad Newman. Yeah. I think I've talked to him." Again
he fell silent and fixed her with that intense stare.

Lisa shifted uneasily in the hard chair.

Suddenly the lieutenant's face softened. He took a last
swipe at his face with the handkerchief and cleared his throat.
"Look, uh, Lisa," he began. "You don't mind if I call you
Lisa, do you?"

Lisa did mind. If he called her by her first name, she
should call him by his and she didn't even know it. She said
nothing.

Lieutenant Cohen was saying, "We know all about Little
Dove Kent and about how her daddy blew himself up along

with the night watchman in that bombing on the Page campus. I talked to her. I talked to all of Professor Silverman's students. She came right out and told me it was her father got blown up that night. First thing—she told me. I didn't even have to ask questions."

Sure, Lisa was thinking. She's no dope. The best defense is a good offense. "Did she say that was the reason she came to school at Addison, because Silverman was here?" Lisa asked.

"No," he said. "What she said was it was a coincidence. That she hadn't even realized he was here."

"And you believed that? Knowing her background? Do you know that her mother committed suicide? She's a strange child who can't seem to relate to others. Frankly, I'm worried about her."

"Look, Miss, uh, Lisa," he said in a voice so patient that she wanted to slug him. "I know you and that reporter were very helpful in that case in Cambridge. I know you're just trying to help now. But we really can do our job."

Lisa squirmed irritably, readying her next attack, but Cohen cut her off.

"You know there was a suicide note?" he asked.

"Yes. I read in the *Globe* that there was a note. Are you sure it was written by Hammer?"

"The crime lab tells me that it was. Perhaps you'd like to see a copy." Cohen remembered how he had been bothered by the tone of the note and the reference to a third victim. But he now had more reason than ever to believe in the note. He had just received information from the FBI that his number-one suspect was eliminated. Danny Connors was dead, killed on September 13, 1971, in the prison revolt at Attica. And he'd just gotten the report that not only was Connors dead, but his only close relatives, his parents and sister, were also dead. Harry McVey had left no survivors. Kent was survived only by his daughter. That left precious few suspects. Of course, there was still Madeline Jennings-Ellison, but he didn't think she was a strong possibility. As for the Kent girl—he hadn't judged her a likely suspect although, of course, one never knew.

"I'd like to see a copy of the note," Lisa said.

Cohen sorted through a pile of papers, fished one out, handed it to her.

Lisa read the note, then looked up at Cohen with a frown. "Murderer of three? I thought only Dove's father and the night watchman were killed in the explosion."

Cohen nodded.

Lisa said, "Dove could have blamed Silverman for her mother's suicide."

"I know about Mrs. Kent's suicide," Cohen said, "but I do not think Dove is the murderer. And the lab reports, as I've said, indicate that the suicide note is genuine. The letter was typed on Hammer's typewriter, which was on the desk in the bedroom where he was found. The signature is his, checked out by the graphics experts in Boston. And the fingerprints on the letter—all his. The pen he used was on the desk, also with his prints on it, just where they should be."

Lisa read the letter again and handed it back. "You're accepting that Hammer did it? You're not going to look any further?"

"Believe me, we will if we have reason to. But so far everything checks out. Everything. The murder and suicide were committed with the same gun. And we know all about the history of these two. Still, we always keep an open mind."

"What about Connors?" Lisa demanded, remembering. "I read that he was sent to prison. Is he still there?"

"Connors is dead, killed in that Attica Prison uprising in 1971." Cohen put his hand out as if to show he wished to be friendly, even though she was a pest. She shook his hand quickly and left.

Driving home, she felt relieved that Cohen knew all about Dove and didn't consider her a suspect. Still, she was worried about the girl. She knew that Dove had come to Addison because of Silverman even though she denied it.

As she headed toward Cambridge, she wished she could go to the River Club and smack a few tennis balls. But she'd let her membership lapse. It was her mother, Anxious Anna, who had paid for her to join in the first place, in the hope that Lisa would meet eligible young men there. Well, she'd met enough eligible young men there, thanks. Too many. Among them had been Chris O'Neil, the tennis pro who was murdered. Anyway, now that she had left her job at Naguchi and was trying to eke by on her slim fellowship at Addison and the few freelance dollars she earned, there wasn't an extra penny, even for tennis balls.

There was something about Hammer's suicide note that bothered her, she thought as she drove, something she didn't quite believe in. Maybe Hammer killed Silverman and then himself. Maybe not. She'd talk to Dove again. See what she could find out. Tomorrow.

Just as Lisa came to the turnpike exit at Newton Corner and looked up at the office building that straddled the turnpike, she remembered that Brad had asked if there was anyone at Addison who had been at Page when the bombing occurred. She turned off at the exit and drove around the hotel and office building. She pulled into the parking lot behind the Newton Public Library and hurried over to a phone booth. She listened to the telephone ringing several times in the office of the Addison Dean of Faculty. Finally a harried voice answered, that of her friend Sonia Janis, an assistant to the dean.

"Sonia, it's Lisa," she said. "I've got to look something up in the faculty files. Will you be there for a while?"

"Lisa," the voice groaned. "I knew I should have gotten out of here. It's almost six. I was just leaving."

"Do me the biggest favor you've ever done me. Wait. I can be there in ten minutes. Please. It's urgent." Lisa didn't think she could possibly wait until morning to follow this up.

"Lisa."

"*Please,*" Lisa begged. "Ten minutes. That's all I ask. You can leave when I get there and I'll lock up."

"Phooey," Sonia exclaimed. "And I was almost out that door."

"You won't be sorry. I'm in your debt. Anything. I'll do anything you ask."

"Shut up and get over here."

Eagerly Lisa drove back toward Braeton.

CHAPTER 18

Thursday Evening, April 26, 1984

Chez Jean was dimly lit and nearly empty. A waiter in a red jacket leaned over their table, trying to light the candle in a pewter holder on the red-checked tablecloth. Each time he lighted a match, the flame blew out, leaving an unpleasant smell of sulphur.

"Here, let me," Sam said amiably. He took the matchbook from the flustered young man, who began to pour water instead. Sam smoothed out the candle wick between his fingers, then moved the burning match patiently around it until the wick caught with a little flare. Lisa watched his hands, big and thick with springy dark hair spreading from under his shirt cuffs over the backs of his hands and fingers. The sight of Sam's capable hands was reassuring, but only slightly. She looked up at his face as he studied the menu—a kind, intelligent face, almost buried in the foaming gray beard.

Sitting flushed and tense, Lisa watched as another waiter poured red wine into the bottom of Sam's wineglass. Sam lifted the glass and tasted, then licked his lips and nodded to the waiter, who filled their glasses and left.

Lisa didn't pick up her glass. She leaned toward Sam, elbows on the table and went on where they had left off. "But I don't understand why you didn't tell me," she said. "Why didn't you say you had been at Page University before Harvard?"

Sam looked at her earnestly. Was he really as emotionally uncomplicated as he seemed? One of the reasons she had found it so easy to feel close to him was that he didn't play games. He said what he thought. He loved her. He'd told her that often in the past few months since they'd met at the Flaggs'. He wanted to marry her. She was the one who wasn't sure. Now his answer seemed sincere. "I hardly ever think about that time. It wasn't a good time for me."

"What do you mean?" she asked. His years at Harvard hadn't been a good time for him either, she was remembering. His research had been unproductive; he hadn't gotten tenure and was forced to leave. Luckily, Addison had hired him, but he was now coming up for tenure, rather late in life. The committee would meet next week to decide if Sam would become a tenured professor. If they decided against him, he would have to leave and, at his age, over fifty, who would hire him? Nothing had been easy for Sam. He often talked to her about his present research. Everything depended on it. But it wasn't going that well.

"Those years at Page were the worst of my life," Sam was saying. "There were problems with my work. Jane left me. She took Eric with her. It's only lately Eric and I are getting acquainted again, beginning to be friends."

Lisa felt a surge of sympathy. She knew about his son Eric. She'd always assumed Jane had left him during those bad years at Harvard. He'd had rotten luck. He was such a vulnerable man.

Earlier this evening, going through the faculty files in the dean of faculty's office, she'd been astonished to see on Sam's record that he had been at Page University in 1968. The faculty files were not secret: they were kept for publicity purposes and open to anyone. She'd been skimming through them so quickly, she'd almost passed his by. She hadn't planned to read his file; she thought she knew everything there was to know about him. But on impulse she pulled it out. She'd been shocked to see that his first appointment after his graduate work at Michigan had been at Page, not at Harvard, as she had thought. She'd known Sam for only a few months, but with a man like Sam, who like a little boy revealed everything about himself, it had seemed long enough to know him well. But, she reminded herself, I've been wrong about men before. Too often.

She realized that Sam had been talking and she hadn't been listening. She tuned in. "Maybe it was a nervous breakdown," Sam was saying, "maybe it wasn't. After Jane left me, I just knew that I couldn't work, not in any way that used my mind. So I up and left Page, before the semester was over. I went back to Michigan, hired on at a logging camp, stayed until I felt ready to go back to my world again, but I just couldn't go back to Page. An old friend of mine was at Harvard. He recommended me for an appointment."

Ordinarily Lisa would have found his story interesting and touching. Now all she wanted to know was what had really happened at Page in 1968. "But you were there when the science center was bombed, weren't you?" she asked.

Sam hesitated before answering, "Yes, I was there."

"Did you know Silverman then?"

"I knew who he was."

"You didn't know him personally?"

"No. But he was a leader of the student activist movement against the war, and he spoke before antiwar groups and staged demonstrations. Everyone knew who he was. His name was always associated with whatever was going on. But, you know me, I wasn't very political, even then."

Lisa nodded. Sam would have been deeply involved in his experiments, unaware of what was going on in the world around him. That was the way he was. She took a sip of her water and then said, "I discovered something this afternoon, something that upset me very much."

"What's that?" Concerned, Sam leaned toward her across the table.

"You remember my talking about my student, Dove Kent, the one whose mother committed suicide?"

Sam nodded.

"Today I found out that she is the daughter of one of the men who was killed in that explosion at Page, James Kent."

"What an odd coincidence."

"I wish I believed it was a coincidence," Lisa said.

"You mean you think she's connected to this murder business?"

"I think it's possible."

"Then you should tell the police."

"I did. I told Lieutenant Cohen."

"What did he say?"

"He already knew. Dove had told him."

"So, forget it." His bushy brows nearly met in concentration.

Was he hiding something? Lisa wondered. Although she watched him closely, she couldn't tell. She went on with her questions. "Dove told me her father was a grad student in science when he died. Was he in your department?"

"No. I didn't know him," Sam said.

"What about the other man involved, Daniel Connors?"

"Connors was a biochemist. I knew him slightly." He shook his head. "A shame. Seemed like a nice boy."

"At the time, did you believe Silverman was involved in the bombing?"

Sam was holding his wineglass waiting to clink it against hers. "I didn't really know," he said in his deep, patient voice that was thick and furred like the backs of his hands. "Naturally, there was a lot of talk on campus at the time. But Silverman denied it. Everyone knew, and he freely admitted his membership in the Anti–Vietnam War Coalition on campus. And he was vice president of SDS. But he insisted he was opposed to violence and he had people to back him up. Plus Lou Hammer to say he had been working with him all that evening. There was no one to say Silverman was lying except for Danny Connors. Connors insisted right through his trial that Silverman was supposed to keep guard outside the science center to keep anyone away from where they were setting the bomb so no one would be hurt. I guess he thought, or his attorney thought, that if he could establish his intent not to harm anyone, they might go easier on him."

Lisa and Sam finally clinked their glasses, and Lisa took a perfunctory sip, but put her glass down and asked, "I suppose you didn't know Hammer then either?"

Sam shook his head. Again Lisa wondered if Sam was telling her everything.

"Funny," she mused. "Silverman was supposed to be such an idealist, but when he felt threatened he did everyone in."

"Fear really peels off the outer layers of a man." Sam drank his wine.

Lisa sipped her wine again, hardly tasting it. She watched

Sam buttering a roll with steady hands. He took a large bite followed by a sip of wine. "And it's funny how it all died away," Lisa continued. "You know, I've been at Addison for almost eight months and I never heard a mention of this story from you or anyone else until the murders brought it all out again."

"Murders?" Sam questioned with a smile.

"You don't think it could be a double murder?"

"The police believe it's murder-suicide. I imagine they've looked into it pretty thoroughly," Sam answered, unperturbed.

"Yes, they do believe it's murder-suicide," Lisa said. "Lieutenant Cohen even showed me a copy of Hammer's suicide note."

They were quiet for a while. Then Lisa said, "But don't you think it's odd that no one around here ever mentioned the explosion or Silverman's possible role in it?"

"Well, not really. Silverman was cleared. I guess most people believed he was innocent, that Connors pulled at him like a drowning man grabbing hold of a swimmer. People forget. Look at Jerry Rubin, alive and well and making bucks on Wall Street."

"Maybe there are some people who didn't forget," Lisa said cryptically.

"You mean Dove Kent?"

Lisa nodded. "Or maybe there's someone else."

Sam shrugged. "Well, I suppose your double murder theory is possible, but murder-suicide has a ring of poetic justice to it. The inevitable working out of fate, the two wrongdoers destroying one another, like a Greek tragedy."

"I don't believe it," Lisa said, staring at him intently, trying to see into him.

"Leave it to the police," Sam said evenly.

Their waiter was bringing covered dishes ceremoniously to the table. He set their breast of duck with orange sauce before them, placing plates of vegetables on the table with a flourish and refilling their wineglasses. Lisa looked down at her food and wished she were hungry. But her appetite had fled. Sam was happily assessing his dinner and picked up his fork and knife with enthusiasm.

"Delicious," he said with a full mouth.

Lisa carefully sliced off a piece of duck, the crisp skin glistening with sauce. She cut off a small piece and put it into her mouth. She wondered if Sam would have told her he'd been at Page in 1968 if she hadn't found out for herself. She'd always thought he was so straightforward. Why, then, did she now feel he was keeping something from her?

She asked casually, "So, did Lieutenant Cohen ask you many questions about life at Page?" If she had to fish, she would fish.

Sam's attention seemed to be completely captured by his food. He looked up. "Not really. I told him I hadn't known Silverman or Hammer, except to nod to—then or now. He wasn't interested in anything else."

Why don't I believe him? Lisa worried. I've never felt this way about him before. She turned her wineglass gently between her palms and looked into the deep red liquid.

Sam put a large, warm hand over one of hers. "Lisa, don't worry so much. Leave it to the police. If Dove's involved, they'll find out."

She looked into his dark brown eyes. Although she had often wondered how deeply she loved him, until now she had never doubted his honesty. He had always made her feel safe, secure. He was reliable. She'd thought he was, anyway. Involuntarily, she shuddered.

His forehead creased with anxiety. "Are you all right?" he asked, kneading her hand with his.

He was so caring, so quick to catch changes in her mood, unlike Brad, who had never seemed to notice such things. Yet she doubted him. Why hadn't he mentioned Page? In a way, his explanation made sense. It was a chapter in his life he wanted to forget. But she still felt he wasn't being completely honest.

Stanifore Street was one of those streets in the South End that had gone way downhill and were on their way up again. Old brownstones, once gracious, then slums, now the objects of loving restoration. It was around eleven when they arrived, and the street was quiet and dark except for an occasional streetlight and the patches of lighted windows. As they drove by number twenty-one, Lisa glimpsed movement and bright colors through gauze curtains of tall first-floor windows. The sounds of music and voices followed them as they parked farther up the street. Sam held her protectively under the elbow as they walked along the uneven brick pavement. Lisa thought again how comfortable she felt being with him, as if she had known him all her life. Isn't that what love was supposed to be?

The moment they entered the first-floor front room of the sagging old townhouse, Sam was taken away from her, almost forcibly, by a woman who seemed to be waiting in the doorway just for him. She was a large woman whose amplitude was concealed under a black one-shouldered dress very much like a toga, and she pounced on Sam as soon as he and Lisa stepped tentatively over the threshold of the high-ceilinged room that seemed to be writhing with people. The woman clasped Sam's arm with both of her hands and dragged him off with an air of authority. Sam gave Lisa a mock-helpless look as he was led away to the dance floor. Lisa smiled, but she felt abandoned. She'd counted on his being by her side when she met Brad and his June. She looked over her shoulder longingly at the dark, empty street behind her.

She stood in the doorway for a while watching the dancers. Brad was nowhere in sight. Once she caught a glimpse of Sam moving backward in the sea of dancers, still looking toward the doorway. He was the only man wearing a suit, Lisa noted. Everyone else, including the young women, wore jeans and T-shirts with the exception of Sam's partner, who was not a young woman at all. The music, loud, heavy on drums, with a monotonous rhythm, was beginning to make her dizzy.

She smiled to herself as she edged along the wall through the living room toward a room beyond. Sam caught up in a scene like this! She could just hear him protesting, "But I don't know how to dance," as the big woman shoved him back and forth. By the time she made it into the smaller, brighter, less crowded room, she was laughing out loud. That Sam. What a pushover he was. And that was the very thing she liked about him. How could she ever distrust a man like that?

A rectangular teak table dominated the dining room. In the center stood a huge bowl half full of punch and piles of plastic glasses as well as large bottles of club soda and ginger ale. Tortilla chips filled several bowls on the table and crunched underfoot.

Lisa poured herself a glass of soda and threw in a couple of ice cubes melting in another bowl. Then she headed for the kitchen in the rear of the house. The kitchen was full of people standing under bright fluorescent lights. She spotted Brad leaning against a soapstone sink, his arm around a woman who gave the impression of being larger than he was, of encompassing him even though she was only standing at his side. Everything about her was round, from her owlish eyes, her round head richly covered with auburn ringlets, to her ample curves barely concealed by a tentlike paisley Indian dress that reflected the color of her hair. The phrase "with a nose like a cherry" flitted through Lisa's head, for the woman's nose was round and pink. Still, she was attractive, with an energy that was apparent even as she stood at Brad's side.

Brad saw Lisa and called out to her with real pleasure.

In an instant the round woman's face changed. She looked at Lisa, and Lisa watched the spectacular alteration of her features from relaxed to wary. The round eyes seemed to grow even rounder with interest. The mouth went from open laughter to a pursed fishlike expression. The body became tenser, tighter. Lisa was aware that no matter what Brad might think of the relationship between this woman and himself, on her part it was proprietary. Brad Newman was her possession, a possession about to be threatened.

Lisa stepped toward them, an awkward smile on her face.

"Lisa, I'm so glad you came." Brad kissed her cheek. "This is June."

"I'm glad you could make it," June said with a composure Lisa admired. Her rich, ripe voice matched her appearance.

"I like your apartment," Lisa said. "The colors are wonderful." She gestured toward the other rooms. "And the paintings. I love them."

June said, "Thanks," and Brad said, "They're June's," both at the same time.

"They're June's paintings," Brad repeated proudly.

"They're great," Lisa said. And they were. Brightly colored

with bold patterns, many of them human figures that the artist had translated into large bright designs.

June wasn't what Lisa had expected at all. She'd expected a pretty, cheerleader-grown-up type, not this large forceful woman. And she'd expected a woman who'd been hurt by a man and was now wary of another relationship. But this woman seemed very sure of herself, as if she knew exactly what her rights were. The way she held her hand on Brad's arm, firmly yet lovingly, said it all. Brad was hers.

A group of young people who seemed the same age as Lisa's students came up to June. "What'd you think of Heinzeker's studio today?" a skinny, bearded man, no more than a boy, asked June. His T-shirt was covered with many-colored paint splotches.

" 'Scuse us," Brad said, grabbing Lisa's hand. "Let's dance. June's back in school, the Museum School," Brad explained as he led her into the living room. "A lot of these people are students, artists."

Lisa caught sight of Sam in the corner of the living room drinking something and talking with the woman in black. Sam waved to her.

"Who's the old man with June's mother?" Brad asked.

"That's June's mother?" Lisa asked in surprise, although she certainly could see the resemblance. "That old man with June's mother is my friend, Sam Harrison," she said.

Then they were caught up in the pounding surge of the music, a part of and yet separate from the rhythms of the other dancers. For a long time they danced that way, in touch with the music and themselves yet not touching each other. Then suddenly the beat changed to a slow, throbbing rhythm. Someone turned the lights lower. Easily she slid into Brad's arms. They danced through the slow number, his chin resting in her hair. When the next one began, fast and sassy, Lisa said, "I need some air. Come. I'll introduce you to the old man."

Sam was standing in the doorway to the dining room, alone now, arms folded across his chest, watching them dance. He put out a hand to Brad and said, "You're Brad. Sam Harrison."

The two men exchanged pleasantries. Then Brad asked Lisa, "Did you get to talk to Lieutenant Cohen?"

"I did," she replied. "But he behaved as if he thought I was a sensation seeker, trying to create a lurid double murder out of an ordinary old murder-suicide."

"Mmm," Brad replied. "Well, I know Cohen and he's a cautious operator. He must have good, solid proof if that's what he believes."

"That's what *I* was trying to tell her," Sam said.

Lisa looked intently at Sam. Was he trying to lead her off the track? But he and Brad were both telling her the same thing—lay off. Just like Lieutenant Cohen. He had told her that he accepted the suicide note as genuine. And he could very well be right. Still, she had to continue to check out her hunch. She'd talk to Dove tomorrow. Somehow, she would have to get the strange girl to tell her what she was hiding.

"Let's go back and talk to June," Brad suggested.

Lisa glanced at her watch. It was after twelve. "I can't, Brad, I've got to get some sleep. I have to be at Addison for a nine o'clock. Please, say good night to her for us."

Brad and Sam shook hands. Just as Lisa and Sam were leaving, June's mother came up to them. "Sam," she called, ignoring Lisa completely. "You're not leaving without a good-bye, after such a lovely evening."

Instantly, Lisa hated her. Her voice, loud and melodious, was the voice of a musical comedy star, an Ethel Merman of the suburbs. A woman who was used to getting what she wanted or complaining in a strong, authoritative voice.

Sam, however, was smiling at her and insisted on introducing her to Lisa as "Fanny, a woman you can really talk to, even over noise like this."

When they were out in the dark street at last, Lisa hurried along silently at Sam's side. Sam was silent, too. Suddenly he stopped so abruptly that she crashed into him. He held her by the elbows. She looked up into his face. Under the yellow light of a streetlamp, his gray hair and beard looked golden, like a lion's mane. "You still care about him," he said angrily.

"Brad?" she asked, as surprised by what he said as by the uncharacteristic show of anger.

"Who do you think? Little Tommy Tucker?" He was unlocking her door. He held the door open and she slid in. He banged it closed with what seemed like unnecessary force and got in the driver's side.

"No," she insisted. "I gave him up. Remember? He was bad for me, like cigarettes," Lisa said as they pulled away from the curb.

Sam was silent as he drove.

"You didn't like him, did you?" Lisa asked.

Sam was staring stonily ahead at the road. "Not particularly."

"Why not?" she asked.

"He's too smooth. Reminds me of that guy Jane ran off with. Anthony Anderson. A smooth talker. Can't be trusted. Smooth-talk you right up until the moment he slides the knife into your heart."

Hunched down into her coat, Lisa shivered. "You must have hated Anthony Anderson, really hated him," she said softly.

Sam snorted, "Hate! I had to get out of there fast—before I killed the guy. Some man to bring up my son." Then as suddenly as it had started, the hate fizzled out of him and he was just poor old Sam for whom nothing ever went right, driving carefully onto Storrow Drive to take her safely home.

In front of her apartment building, he took her in his arms. She tried to relax into the gentle swells of passion that she usually felt with him, but she couldn't. He sensed her lack of response and moved away from her. He stared moodily down at the steering wheel.

"I'm tired, Sam," she said apologetically.

She saw the questions in his eyes, but he said nothing.

She guessed that he had hoped she would ask him in tonight. She thought of the times they had made love, the power of his gentleness. "I'm sorry, I . . . ." she began as he opened the car door for her.

"It's all right," he said quickly.

He walked her to her apartment door, as he always did, gave her a quick kiss on the cheek, and was gone.

The telephone was ringing as she walked into her apartment.

Brad's voice. "Hi, Lisa. I just wanted to thank you for coming. It felt right, just being with you. I wanted to tell you so."

So he had felt it, too. That special something between them was still there. "Thanks for asking me—us. But why are you calling now? It's almost one."

"I've been trying for the past half hour. You said you were

going right home." He hesitated and then said, "Lisa, I'm . . . look . . . dammit, I'm worried about you."

"You're what?"

"Look—that guy, he's old enough to be your father. Fanny's interested in him. Y'know, June's mother, Fanny."

"Oh, so you're calling to warn me off, give Fanny a chance."

"Lisa. For God's sake. Look. You know how vulnerable you are. Because of your father and everything."

He meant because of himself. Lisa was quiet, remembering how at one time she had told Brad everything, about how her father, Absent Abe, had left her and her mother, just walked out on them when Lisa was only five, about how lonely they had been. She had told Brad things she'd never told anyone before. But then it was different. Then Brad had held her in his arms, tried to make her forget. Now . . . "It's none of your damn business," she exploded.

"I'm sorry. I guess I shouldn't have called."

She didn't contradict him.

There was silence and then Lisa asked, "Would June be mad if she knew you were calling me?"

"No. Of course not. Why should she be?"

Silence again.

Then Brad said, "Look, Lisa, I'll be honest with you. Things just aren't as they should be between June and me. She wants more than I, I . . . I mean, I don't know. Maybe it's because I'm still hung up on you, but I can't, I don't feel the way I should . . . I mean, maybe you and I should . . ."

Lisa let him go on as long as she could stand it. "You're back at a place I remember very well. Only this time it's you and June instead of you and me."

"Lisa, you just don't understand . . ."

"I don't know if I'm hearing you right. But before you go any further, I want to say that I'll never give you the chance to hurt me again."

After she finished talking to Brad, she couldn't fall asleep. What was this tingling she felt from head to toe when she thought about Brad's voice on the phone laced with emotion? "I'm still hung up on you. Hung up on you. Hung up on you." His words played over and over again in her mind like a stuck record.

Of course she couldn't want Sam when she felt this way about Brad. How could she? And she was worried about the change in her evaluation of Sam's character. His dislike of Brad had been real and very strong. She had never before seen him so angry. Beneath his passive surface were feelings he hid very well. Maybe she didn't know him at all. Why had he never told her he was at Page? Had he been, in some way, connected to Silverman and Hammer?

When she finally slept, Dove's hideous laughter rang through disjointed dreams of the grotesque.

CHAPTER 19

Friday Morning, April 27, 1984

The English Department lounge was crowded as usual this morning. 1968 BOMBING LEADS TO ADDISON MURDER-SUICIDE, the headline screamed from the morning *Globe* opened up next to the coffee urn on the refectory table. The vase of forsythia was back on the table, the flowers bowing gently in the breeze from the open windows.

Lisa poured coffee into a Styrofoam cup and listened to the heated discussion in progress.

"The late sixties was an era of freedom," Madeline was arguing in righteous tones from the sofa. She'd kicked off her sandals. Her bare feet were up on the coffee table. "I was an undergrad at Brandeis then. We thought we could change everything. It was an era of hope."

"Hope," Professor Froming said with disgust, looking at Madeline's feet. "Irresponsibility, I'd call it. An era of irresponsibility." He sipped from a rose-painted cup.

"Just what were you, all of you, trying to accomplish?" Mary Reardon asked Madeline earnestly, ignoring Froming. Mary was sitting in a canvas sling chair in the corner, wearing one of her tweed suits and her sensible shoes. Catching Lisa's eye, she smiled.

"We were trying to make a better world," Madeline said with feeling. "We were angry that young men were being sent to Vietnam to die because of some stupid domino theory. We saw blacks and poor people treated like shit while huge amounts of money went into military buildup. Individuals were standing up against authority, refusing to pay taxes that went for military spending, refusing to be drafted."

"It does sound like a time of hope," Mary said.

"Irresponsible acts," Froming repeated, "carried out in the name of freedom. Attempts by malcontents to destroy a world they wouldn't or couldn't accept."

Madeline responded bitterly, "Most of us wanted to improve the world, not destroy it."

"Most?" Froming questioned with sarcasm. And when Madeline began to reply, he raised his voice above hers, "I think not. Most of you were crazed with power." He shivered, remembering. "A spoiled generation, too indulged to listen to reason. In 1968 it was almost impossible to teach. Students thought they had more to teach us than we had to teach them."

"Maybe we did," Madeline said.

Froming turned from her and seemed to be addressing the room at large in his dry, thin voice. "Fortunately, we now have an age of reason in which true scholarship may be pursued. Are you ready, Applewhite?" He turned on his precise heel and exited.

Bob Applewhite, sitting at the refectory table, hurriedly pushed his papers together. He followed Froming out, papers fluttering, looking neither right nor left.

"If that's true scholarship, count me out," Madeline said,

closing her book with a slap. "That man is so narrow he'd fit into a crack in the wall."

Mary laughed her slow, throaty laugh. "It's wonderful the way you always say exactly what you mean, Madeline."

Madeline looked at her sharply, not knowing how to take the remark.

"I'm not being sarcastic," Mary said quickly. "I mean it. You see, I'm often afraid of telling people what I really think. And Lisa here is always the soul of tact. But you aren't afraid to speak your mind, even to the chairman of the department."

Madeline must have decided she really was being complimented. She said, "It's because I understand the little concessions we are constantly making to those in authority or those we think are in authority. And I've decided I will not do it anymore. Most of these so-called authorities are phonys. Like Silverman—mouthing revolution, then letting those poor guys down and buying off that fool Hammer to keep his bloody secret."

"I agree," Mary said. "We must judge by the deed, not the posturing." She headed for the door. "Excuse me. I must telephone the chairman of the James Joyce conference to find out when my panel is meeting."

When Mary had left the room, Lisa said carefully, "You didn't always feels such disgust for Silverman, did you?" Madeline seemed so tough. It was hard to imagine her letting those defenses down for anyone, especially for Silverman. Lisa wanted to find out if she really had. She expected Madeline would answer her by telling her to mind her own business.

But Madeline didn't seem annoyed by Lisa's prying. She shrugged with resignation. "It's true," she said. "And I guess everybody knows about it by now. There was a time—a short time—when I thought I was in love with him. I believed the things he told me." She gave a short laugh. "You should've heard him. He spoke of the miracle of our finding one another, of love. And I, poor fool that I was, I believed him, for a while. Because I wanted to. But I found out about him— the hard way. And now I'm not even surprised at the monstrousness of his behavior back in '68. I always wondered about the strange relationship between him and Lou Hammer. Now it makes sense." She shook her head slowly. "But that Hammer should have killed him and then himself. Wow."

"I'm not sure I believe in that murder-suicide theory," Lisa said.

Mary reentered the room. "The line is engaged," she sighed. "I think he's taken the receiver off the hook." She poured coffee.

Madeline was looking at Lisa in surprise. "The newspapers say the police have checked it out and they believe it. You don't think Hammer did it?" she asked.

Lisa shrugged. "It could have been a third person killed them both."

As Lisa was speaking, Professor Froming and Professor Fletcher came into the lounge followed by Bob Applewhite.

"I suggest we leave this investigation to the police and go about our business," Froming said irritably. He poured more coffee into his flowered china cup.

Ignoring him, Fletcher asked Lisa, "Did I hear you say you didn't agree with the police that it was murder-suicide?"

"That's right," Lisa said.

"May I ask why?" Fletcher's eyes were round with fear or surprise.

Everyone was watching Lisa, and it occurred to her that she

had no really sensible explanation to offer for her suspicions. She certainly did not want to mention her fears about Dove. "I don't know," she stammered, "just feelings I have. I have to think about it some more, check out a few things," she finished vaguely. Then she turned to Froming and said, "You knew Professor Hammer better than any of us. Do you think he was capable of killing Professor Silverman and then himself?"

There was a silence in the room. Everyone looked toward Froming. Lisa had a chance to glance quickly around at the others, to gauge the expressions on their faces. Mary had that look of irony on her face, but it had solidified into something like distaste. Madeline looked belligerent. Bob Applewhite looked even paler and more frightened than usual. Fletcher seemed very interested.

Froming was looking down his nose at her. For someone so small, he managed that expression of disdain with great confidence. "I am a professor of English Literature. I do not go around trying to be a police inspector." He spat out the final syllables, but delicately, like someone in a fancy restaurant who has put a slightly rancid piece of fish into his mouth. Then he turned and headed for the door. Mary put her hand over her mouth playfully, as if to suppress a giggle, and winked at Lisa. When Froming had disappeared, she said to Lisa, "Sounds as if you suspect someone."

"Do you?" Bob Applewhite asked, his mouth a perfect O.

Lisa felt she had said enough. Too much, perhaps. Everyone was waiting for her reply. "Oh, I don't know," she said. "C'mon, Mary, let's have some lunch."

Lisa and Mary squeezed into a corner table at the rear of the cafeteria where they could have some privacy. Lisa unloaded her salad and iced tea onto the formica table and slid her tray onto the table next to theirs. She watched enviously as Mary placed her beef stew, mashed potatoes, strawberry ice cream, and coffee in front of her. Mary never gave a thought to her weight. She said that Americans were obsessed with thinness. And it was true, Lisa thought. She knew she was obsessed with it.

"What a week," she said as Mary sat beside her. "I've been dying to talk to you."

"Don't say 'dying,' " Mary said. She poured cream into her coffee and shook in two packets of sugar. "Not this week."

"How was your grilling by the police?" Lisa asked.

"I thought Lieutenant Cohen was going to ask me for a date," Mary said. "He thought everything I said was immensely funny."

"Like what?"

Mary leaned toward her, laughing. "I told him Silverman was a leprechaun-sized lecher. He loved it. Local color, isn't that what you call it?"

Lisa joined in the laughter until she remembered he was dead. "I can't believe he's dead," she said. He'd been one of their favorite jokes.

Mary shrugged, took a spoonful of ice cream.

"Hey, that's dessert," Lisa chided.

"Why? Why does it have to be?"

Lisa laughed again.

"Also," Mary began, returning to her stew, "Lieutenant Cohen was very interested in my background."

"You mean because you're Irish and Danny Connors, the guy who was convicted of murder in the Page bombing, was Irish?" Lisa had already thought of the coincidence of their both being Irish.

"Exactly." Mary laughed. "Grasping at straws, they are."

"So what did you tell them?" Lisa asked, trying to sound casual although she was feeling a tingle of concern because she, also, had made the connection.

If Mary was aware of Lisa's concern, she didn't show it. "I explained to them that Northern Ireland where Daniel Connors came from and the Republic of Ireland, where I live, are two separate countries. Connors came from Derry in Northern Ireland and studied at Queen's College in Belfast. I was born and brought up outside of Dublin, did my academic work at Trinity College, and never even heard of Daniel Connors. It's like saying that you must know someone in Philadelphia, at the University of Pennsylvania, because you're an American."

Lisa nodded, relieved. "Had you ever been to Londonderry?"

"Once," Mary said, "when my Mum and Dad were alive." Her eyes grew misty. She asked, "What about you?"

"Me?"

"Your grilling?"

"Oh, nothing interesting. But I went back to talk to them yesterday afternoon."

Mary's auburn eyebrows rose, taking her perfect widow's peak with them. "You did?"

Lisa lowered her voice. "About Dove. I saw her Monday. I wanted to talk to you. I'm worried about her."

"That's why you went to the police?" Mary asked.

"I'm worried that she's connected to the murders in some way."

"Why do you think that?"

Lisa said in a half-whisper, "She hated Silverman, Mary. I found out her father was one of the men killed in that explosion at Page in 1968. She was in my office Monday, the day

Silverman's appointment to the Finstermann Chair was announced in the *Addison News,* and all that hate just exploded out of her. You know, I've been telling you how she was fascinated by him, that sometimes the only way I could get her to talk to me was by bringing him up. Well, it's not because she had a crush on him, as we guessed, or anything like that. She hated him.'"

Mary shook her head and gave Lisa that gentle, ironic smile of hers. "Darling, you are overreacting by half a league. She might have hated him or whatever . . ."

"I know hate when I see it."

"All right. Hate, then. That doesn't mean she murdered the man."

"I've got so much to tell you, I don't know where to begin," Lisa said. "Yesterday I called my ex-boyfriend, Brad Newman, you know, the reporter for the *Globe.* He arranged for me to look through some 1968 *Globe* files, and . . ."

Mary's mouth fell open. "I thought you were all over that."

Lisa put her hand on Mary's, causing a heaping forkful of stew poised between plate and mouth to fall onto the table. "Listen, dammit, what I found out from the newspaper files was that Dove's father was one of the men who bombed the science center at Page University in 1968. He died in the explosion."

"No. You're not serious."

"So, you see, Dove blamed Silverman for his death. She had reason to hate him, to want to kill him."

Mary just stared at her.

"She could have killed him, then killed Hammer because Hammer got Silverman off and so he'd be a natural to take the rap."

"I just do not believe this," Mary said, looking stunned. "I read the paper. It said the police are almost convinced Louis Hammer killed Silverman and then killed himself."

"They've been wrong before, the police."

Mary shook her head, but now she looked worried.

"The girl could be deranged," Lisa said anxiously. "She's had such a tragic life. I'm really worried about her. Yesterday, when I told her I knew about her father's death, she got hysterical, ran out of my office."

"Did you tell the police about her father?" Mary asked.

"Yes, Lieutenant Cohen said Dove had already told him."

Mary looked relieved. "Well, then, that's a good sign. At least she's being honest with them."

Lisa nodded. "About her father, about who he was and how he died. After all, she must've known they'd find out. But she knows something more than she's telling. I'm sure of it."

"Do you think I should try to talk to her?" Mary suggested. "I feel that lately she's been willing to talk to me about her feelings. Ever since I told her that I, too, lost my parents when I was young, we've been talking about what it felt like to be all alone."

"If you think you could, it might really help," Lisa said in relief. "I looked for her today, and I tried calling her, but I couldn't find her. And I'm going away for the weekend with my mother to visit my Aunt Ruth. I'll try again the beginning of the week. In the meantime, if you can find out anything, let me know."

"I'll talk to her," Mary promised. She was soaking up the last of her gravy with a piece of bread.

Lisa's jaws were tired from crunching lettuce. She watched Mary enjoying the last of her substantial lunch.

"So tell me about your suddenly calling the old boyfriend," Mary said. "And what about Sam?"

"Oh, Mary, Brad is so . . . I don't know. All I have to do is look into those evil eyes of his and I forget there ever was Sam." As she said this, Lisa thought of her discovery that Sam had been at Page in 1968 and felt a pang of anxiety, but she didn't want to talk about it.

"Evil? Isn't that a bit overstated?" Mary asked.

"Brad will never be true," Lisa said.

Mary got up. They clanked crockery back onto their trays. "If you feel for him, Lisa darling . . ." They put their trays on the dirty dish cart.

"What?" Lisa asked.

"You've got to follow your heart."

"Is that a wise old Irish saying?"

"A wise new one," Mary said. "You'd better give him another try."

"You sound like my mother."

"Your mother! I don't want to sound like your mother. Don't you call her Anxious Anna because she's always worrying about you?"

"That's right. But she isn't anxious about Brad. In fact, she's quite taken with him. Do you know they call each other on the phone?"

"Aha. Maybe he's secretly in love with her," Mary said. "Wasn't there a French movie about that—daughter's beau falling for her mum?"

Lisa thought. "Well, I don't know. But if not, there will be."

They laughed.

Lisa said, "I'm very attracted to him, but I don't trust him."

Mary nodded wisely. "Another try," she repeated.

* * *

Lisa was just leaving her apartment to pick up Anna for the drive to New Hampshire that evening when the telephone rang. She hurried back in and picked it up.

It was Brad. "I have to see you," he said.

"You don't *have* to see me. You *want* to see me, to see if you'd rather be torturing me than June. I don't want to see you," she lied, "and I sure don't have to if I don't want to."

"Let me remind you of something." He paused for emphasis. "*You* called *me*."

Lisa was quiet for a moment. What he said was true. She had called him, and she knew that she could have gotten the information about Kent at any library.

Brad went on, "I've been thinking about you for a long time now, staying up nights seeing your face. But I didn't call you. You called me."

"I'm sorry," she said, without knowing what exactly it was she was sorry about.

"D'you think that's fair?" His voice was plaintive.

"I don't know," she said, really trying to think about what was fair in this case. "I'll have to think about it. Right now I'm late. I'm picking up Anna to take her to her sister's for the weekend.

"We'll talk next week, then," Brad said.

She should have just said good-bye as she'd planned to, and not put it off until next week. But he was right. She *had* called him. It was as if she were two people, one fighting the other in underhanded ways.

Driving to Anna's apartment in Brookline, she remembered what she'd forgotten to do. She'd meant to call Dove again. Well, maybe Mary would talk to her. She'd try to put it out of her mind until Monday.

CHAPTER 20

Monday Morning, April 30, 1984

Lisa concentrated on breathing. In through the nose. Deep. Now out through the mouth. Open mouth, empty those lungs. Now fill 'em up again. In, out. In, out. Let the legs take care of themselves. At least she was still moving. Two miles. The best yet. It wasn't quite light. Early dawn, mist above the river. Leaves shyly unfurling on the trees. Every breath seemed an achievement, every footfall a miracle. And there was her apartment building looming out of the mist like the bow of a ship across Greenough Boulevard. Only a hundred yards ahead. Just don't think about pain. Think about that warm shower, that great cup of coffee. Those burnt-up calories.

Behind her she sensed rapid motion, then heard tires skimming on pavement. Now gravel. Very fast. Very close. Half-turning to see, she forgot the pain of her body as her heart lurched in a somersault of fear. The car was almost upon her, bearing down, off the road now, on the gravel shoulder behind her and hurtling toward her. No lights on, it seemed like a fragment of a nightmare. A matter of seconds only before impact. No place to run. No escape. Unless . . . She threw herself at the outcropping of shoulder-high rock between her and the river. Springing up as high as she could, head first, she grazed the rock with her knees. She heard the sickening crash of metal against rock in the instant that her right ankle slammed against the ledge. Then she was lying face down on the spongy river bank, tall grass and cattails prickling her face and arms and legs. She heard the grating noise of the car scraping free of the rock and then the gunning of the engine as the car roared into high gear and sped away.

Pulling herself up on the rock, Lisa saw the dark shape moving swiftly off in the direction of Fresh Pond Parkway. Heart pounding so rapidly she could hardly breathe, she assessed damages. Knees scraped, but not too badly. Ankle painful with a gash that was bleeding, but not profusely. Could be worse. She'd expected worse. She crossed the street at a slow, limping run, looking urgently in the direction the car had taken, and continued running to her building. It wasn't until she was inside her apartment sitting in the kitchen with a towel pressed to the cut on her ankle that she allowed herself to think about how close she had come. And to form the words in her mind: Someone tried to kill me. Kill me or put me out of commission—for a good long time.

She dialed the Cambridge police. As the phone rang, she decided what she'd do. She'd ask for Lieutenant Gibson, the competent woman who'd been in charge of the Chris O'Neil murder case. But the man who answered the phone told her that Lieutenant Gibson wasn't expected in until nine.

Lisa took a deep breath. "I'll call her later, then. But I do want to report a . . . an incident on Greenough Boulevard." Lisa proceeded to describe what had happened. "And the car crashed into the rock as I dove over it and out of the way." Even to her own ears it sounded like a Superwoman comic.

She wasn't surprised at the lack of interest she perceived in the policeman's voice, especially when she couldn't tell him the color or make of car—except that it was old and dark.

"Sure. We'll check on it, Miss. Just come into the station and file a report."

On her way to Braeton, she looked suspiciously at every car that came near her on the road. But she had to deal with nothing more dangerous than the usual pushiness and incompetence of the morning rush-hour commuters.

Waiting in Lieutenant Cohen's office, she felt her whole body trembling.

Lieutenant Cohen came in shortly. She told him what had happened. "I'm frightened," she concluded. "The person driving that car was trying to kill me."

Cohen's forehead wrinkled with sympathy. "Would you like a cup of coffee?" he asked.

"No. Thank you. I'm all right. But the person in that car was trying to kill me," she repeated. "And I think it must be because I've been asking questions about the Silverman-Hammer case."

"This happened in Cambridge, you say? Did you report it to the Cambridge police?" he asked.

"Yes. I did. Immediately. But I don't think they took it very seriously. I'm going to call back and talk to Lieutenant Gibson, whom I know."

"I take it seriously. Very seriously, indeed," Cohen assured her. "However, I have told you my thinking on the Silverman-Hammer deaths. The evidence points to murder-suicide. Therefore, I'm inclined to doubt whether the incident had anything to do with the case. Incidents like this between runners and motorists and between bicyclists and motorists occur constantly in Boston and surrounding communities."

"You mean motorists who aim for and try to kill runners and bicycle riders?" she asked, unbelieving.

He nodded. "Unfortunately, there are a few people with a kind of king-of-the-road mentality that makes them try to rid the roads of nuisances who don't belong there, like joggers and bicyclists. The other possibility is a motorist getting a charge out of trying to scare you."

Lisa shook her head emphatically, remembering the sound of metal clanging against stone in the moment her body was flying over the rock barrier. If she hadn't been next to the rocks, he would have run her down for sure. She shuddered.

"Can you describe the car?" he asked.

"Just that it was old and dark-colored. But there must be some evidence on that rock—paint or something. It hit pretty hard."

"Okay, I'll call Lieutenant Jencks over in Cambridge Traffic, get him to send someone over to check it out. I'll get back to you if we find out anything. But I think it was probably one of those freaks and you just happened to be in the wrong place at the wrong time."

They shook hands. It would be a long time before she dared to jog again. Damn. Just when she finally broke two miles. Her injured ankle throbbed when she put weight on it.

As she limped to the door, Hughes was coming up the stairs. He held the heavy wooden door for her. She gave him only a curt nod, didn't even wait to see his practiced smile. Leaning against the door, he watched her go down the stairs, favoring her good foot.

"You have a visitor?" he asked his superior as he sat at his desk. "A visitor with tight jeans, maybe, and a bum leg?"

"Car nearly got her when she was running this morning. She thinks someone is trying to kill her," Cohen said.

Hughes whistled through his teeth. "For real?" he asked.

"It doesn't make much sense," Cohen said, "unless . . ."

"Unless?"

"Unless she's onto something. Or someone thinks she is." He handed Hughes a slip of paper. "Here. Call Jencks in Cambridge. Ask him to check it out and tell him it's urgent."

"Urgent?" Hughes was surprised.

"If someone's taking aim at her, we'd better find out and fast. How's your canvass going?"

"Finished. Saw the pregnant lady. Well, she's not pregnant anymore. I talked to her at Braeton General. She just had a baby. She was up all night the night Hammer was shot, timing labor pains. Saw nothing. No suspicious characters. No one at all. And she was looking out the window. Her apartment faces the front walk. The only other person I hadn't talked to, the guy on vacation, came back last night. Nothing."

"Hmm." Cohen was leaning way back in his chair. "If it weren't for our Ms. Davis . . ."

Lisa arrived at the Addison parking lot just before 9:00. Ordinarily, she would have come in an hour later, right before her 10:00 class. Now she backed her car into a shaded spot at the far end of the lot next to a gray van. She lay back in the driver's seat. She was still shaking. Fear for her life was a new feeling.

In the next hour she watched twenty or thirty cars arrive, among them most of the English faculty and grad students as well as several people from the Philosophy Department. The two departments shared the building and parking lot. Professor Froming was the first to arrive, parking his orange-red

VW, the color of tomato soup, in the space nearest the gravel walk. Then Edith Waks pulled up in a shiny black compact car and parked next to him. Lisa saw her hurry on slender high heels toward the ivy-covered building.

After several cars of colors and makes that didn't interest her parked, she watched an old dark green car enter the lot and pull into a space. In a few moments Professor Ted Flagg emerged from the driver's side and marched toward the building, his body stiff, his face set in anger. When he'd disappeared from view, a short plump woman wearing a black tentlike dress and sandals got out. She was wiping her face. She blew her nose and reached into the back seat to pick up a mountain of books. Then she trudged down the slope toward the Languages Building. Lisa slid farther down in her seat as Tessa Flagg passed by. An unhappy marriage, and Tessa seemed to get fatter and fatter. When she too was out of sight, Lisa got out and walked over to the Flaggs' car. She inspected it carefully. There were a few old dents, rusted over, but no fresh scrapes, nothing to indicate an encounter with a rock on Greenough Boulevard early this morning.

Lisa went back and sat in her car. A few more cars entered the parking lot, among them another VW, this one light blue like her own, driven by Mary. It was almost ten now. Lisa hurried over and they walked toward the English building together.

Mary seemed to be her usual outgoing self. As they approached the English building she looked sideways at Lisa and said, "Something wrong? You look a bit peaked."

As usual Lisa was cheered by the lilt of Mary's voice. "A bit," she replied. "Someone tried to kill me this morning."

Mary stopped and grabbed her arm. "Come on, now. You're putting me on." On her lips, the slang sounded like a line from a play, but Lisa didn't joke about it as she usually did. "Wish I were," she replied morosely. "I'm really scared."

"Why would anyone?" Mary asked, aghast. "How?"

"Someone tried to run me down this morning when I was jogging."

"You're sure? It wasn't some drunk?"

"No. It was meant for me, all right. Although the police think it was a nut."

"Maybe they'll find the nut," Mary said.

Lisa almost laughed this time. Mary was so funny when she tried to adopt American slang, like "nut." She pronounced the word so carefully, giving it real importance. "Nah. They'll never find the nut. They won't even try, even though the driver smashed into some rocks and must've left a lot of evidence."

"It must have been a crazy," Mary said.

This time Lisa did laugh out loud.

"What's so funny?" Mary asked.

"You're doing it again, talking slang as if it were the Queen's English."

Impulsively, Mary hugged her. "You sure you're all right, darling?" she asked fondly.

The usual coffee drinkers were gathered in the lounge as Lisa and Mary entered. Lisa announced her near-accident to the group at large and watched for reactions. Bob Applewhite turned predictably paler. Professor Froming got that nauseated look and expressed his belief that the incident was unrelated to the murder-suicide. Madeline seconded Froming's statement with a diatribe against the macho attitude that the roads belonged to the automobile. Edith Waks looked harassed, sorting her sheafs of papers to hand out. Hurrying back to her office to prepare the Xerox machine for action, she muttered, "When will we ever get back to normal?"

Lisa called Lieutenant Gibson from the pay phone outside the English office. Gibson echoed Cohen's opinion that the driver had probably been one of those motorists who enjoyed attacking joggers. "But I'll call Lieutenant Jencks, get it checked out," she promised.

Professor John Fletcher rocked back and forth on the lecture platform as he droned on about the relationship between Walt Whitman's newspaper articles for the *Brooklyn Eagle* and his *Leaves of Grass.* Who cares? Lisa thought. He seemed to be leaving out anything that might be interesting. But she doubted that she could concentrate on anything, even on something interesting, right now. She kept thinking about how Silverman's death had given Fletcher his big chance. Sure, a good third of the students present were drowsing in their seats as the eager man went on and on mercilessly. Still, his sudden elevation to teaching a major course could not help but be a step in the right direction for his career. Lisa wondered just how calculating John Fletcher was and how badly he might have wanted Silverman out of the way. But how could that explain the sudden demise of Professor Hammer?

Lisa sighed and made some of her favorite doodles, circles with triangular hats, on her notebook paper. Someday she'd see a shrink and try to figure out just what these doodles meant. Experimentally, she drew a mustache on one of the circles. Her father? Absent Abe had had a mustache. She remembered the tickly feel of it when he kissed her. He was in the hospital. She didn't want to see him. Why should she? He had left them, Anxious Anna and her. He hadn't come back until he was dying. She was ten. She didn't want him to kiss her.

Lisa spotted Dove sitting alone at the back of the room. She put her pencil down as she came to a decision. She would follow Dove, see where she lived, see if somewhere around her place there was an old dark-colored car with fresh scrapes from an early-morning murder attempt. Dove had reacted strangely when they discussed her father's death. More than strangely. The girl had been hysterical. Lisa remembered that she had told Dove she didn't believe in the murder-suicide theory. Maybe the girl was trying to stop her before she found out anything more.

Following Dove was easier said than done. Lisa was stopped by several students on her way out of the lecture hall. They wanted to know everything from whether they were responsible for Fletcher's lecture on the hour exam next week to whether they could hand in their papers late because of . . . Lisa had long ago stopped listening to the reasons; they were so predictably outrageous.

By the time she got outside, she could just see Dove's pale head bent over a bicycle at the far side of the parking lot. Lisa got to her car and drove at a distance behind Dove as she pedaled across campus and, disappointingly, chained her bike to the rack in front of the student center, one of the oldest buildings on campus, weathered brick covered with decades of ivy.

Dove was inside for a long time. Both Lisa's watch and the rumbling in her stomach told her that lunchtime was coming and going. She wished she had had the foresight to pack, at very least, a banana before leaving her apartment this morning. And her ankle was throbbing. Maybe she should have it

X-rayed. She tried to read, but couldn't because she had to look up every time the door of the building opened.

Shortly before two, Dove came out, alone as usual. She hopped on her bike and took off without a backward glance. Lisa followed Dove through the open iron gate of the campus and down the wide main road that led to Braeton Center. Past the train station, an old stone building with arched entrances. Past the post office at the edge of the center. Past the new shiny brick Georgian apartment buildings, where, Lisa knew, Professor Hammer had died. Right before the center of town Dove turned onto Lowell Street and rode past the old Victorian houses, now student rooming houses and off-campus fraternities, with sagging front porches and cupolas that needed paint.

Lisa knew Lowell Street well. Sam lived on Lowell Street in one of the garden apartments that had been built around a cul-de-sac at the end of the street. Dove didn't slow down, but headed straight for the apartment complex. Lowell Street was teeming with life, students sitting on front steps drinking beer out of paper cups so that the police wouldn't stop them; students hurrying to and from the university with books and Frisbees.

The street was parked up on both sides. Lisa stopped behind another VW that was pulling out of a tiny space. Its driver, who looked like a fraternity boy, honked in comradely greeting. Lisa didn't reciprocate. She hoped Dove wouldn't turn around and spot her. But Dove seemed to be concentrating on where she was going. She slowed down as she approached the first of the low brick buildings, rode onto the sidewalk on the right-hand side of the street, and coasted slowly. In front of the third unit, she stopped. It was number six, Sam's building. Lisa watched in surprise as Dove rode up the concrete walk to Sam's front door, got off, leaned her bike against the railing, and rang the bell.

In a matter of moments the door swung open. Sam held the door open as Dove preceded him into the apartment.

As the door closed behind them, Lisa felt overwhelmed by the suspicions about Sam that had begun when she looked at his file in the dean of faculty's office last Thursday. Sam had never told her he had been at Page. What else hadn't he told her? She tried to remember how he'd reacted when she talked about Dove last Thursday night at dinner. She had talked to him about the girl often before; about her mother's suicide, her fascination with Silverman, her strange, guarded manner. He'd never indicated in any way that he knew her. And when she told him of her discovery that Dove's father had been killed in the bombing at Page, he seemed surprised. He said he hadn't even known Jim Kent and had known Daniel Connors, the other man involved in the bombing, only slightly. Yet Sam seemed to know a lot about the trial of Daniel Connors. Strange that he'd never mentioned anything about Page to her.

What could Dove possibly have to do with Sam? Lisa wondered as she waited restlessly, her stomach complaining. She breathed in sharply as she had a new thought. If Dove were the murderer, could she be planning to harm Sam? Kill him? But if she had killed Silverman because he was responsible for her father's death, and then Hammer because he had saved Silverman's neck and would do to take the rap, why would she want to kill Sam? He hadn't anything to do with the bombing at Page. Had he? Or did Dove think he had?

Suddenly Lisa sat up straight and opened the car door.

Fears for Sam's safety crowded out all her other fears. She started to get out just as the door to his apartment opened and Sam, very much alive, came out onto the front stoop with Dove. Lisa ducked down, closing the door softly. They were talking in low voices. Lisa couldn't hear what they were saying, but the tone was argumentative. Sam went inside and closed the door. Dove swung onto her bike and pedaled by rapidly, head down. Lisa just caught a glimpse of her face streaming with tears.

Lisa watched Dove reach the end of the street and make a left turn, away from Braeton Center. Taking a last look at Sam's closed front door, Lisa made a U-turn and followed the girl. Dove rode past Braeton General Hospital, a low modern building set back from the road, and continued for about a mile before turning off onto a dirt road. Lisa drove a little way beyond Dove's turnoff until she found a place where she could not be seen from the road, but she could see Dove's road through the trees. She parked and waited. Dove could be in there for the rest of the day. Lisa daydreamed about a medium-rare hamburger with raw onions, lots of ketchup, and a side of fries. She had all she could do to stay put. Ten more minutes, she told herself, and I'm off to the nearest fast-food oasis.

She didn't have to wait for ten minutes. Dove reappeared, her bicycle laden with books, and turned toward Braeton Center. She sped away, back to the Addison Library, no doubt. When Dove was out of sight, Lisa drove down her dirt road, through a pine-scented woods to a little cabin in a clearing. There was a driveway next to the house, but no garage. Lisa got out and walked all around the house. There was no car hidden, no tire tracks in the soft earth. If Dove were the one who had tried to run her down this morning, it was not in a car that she kept here.

As Lisa drove back to Cambridge, she remembered that tonight was supposed to be a special night. She'd invited Sam to dinner to celebrate the three-month anniversary of their meeting. She stopped at the Star Market on Mount Auburn Street and without enthusiasm picked up the fixings for a celebratory dinner.

CHAPTER 21

Monday Evening, April 30, 1984

Sam arrived right at 7:30. He brought champagne. They sat side by side on Lisa's new sofa, their knees touching as he uncorked it. Lisa held her right ankle out stiffly. She'd wrapped an ace bandage around it.

"Oh!" she cried involuntarily as the cork flew up to the ceiling, hitting with a thud, like the sound of a body falling, leaving a gray mark on the plaster.

Sam held the champagne bottle in a kitchen towel, poured quickly before it foamed over. Lisa watched his face. A look of intense concentration froze his features into a death mask. Would he tell her that Dove Kent had been to see him only a few hours ago?

"Happy anniversary," he said. "Three months today." He leaned toward her, holding his glass out for a toast. She smelled his cleanness. A hint of shampoo and some spicy after-shave lotion. He had showered, shaved, put on clean clothes for her.

They clinked glasses. "To our mutual friends. Thanks be to them," he said, looking at her fondly.

"The Flaggs. Long may they wave," she said, seeing in her

mind Tessa's tear-stained face. They had met at the Flaggs'. Ted Flagg, an instructor in eighteenth-century literature and the director of the freshman writing program, was the son of an old friend of Sam's.

They sipped. She handed him the plate of deviled eggs as she said casually, "So, how was your day?"

He took a delicate bite of an egg and didn't, she noticed, meet her eye. "Fine."

"Uh, what did you do today?" she asked.

"Worked all day. Taught my class at four."

"So, were you at Addison all day, then?"

He looked at her keenly. With a touch of suspicion? "No, I worked at home until after lunch. Then I went in to the lab. Why?"

She put her glass on the table. "No reason, really. I just wanted to hear about your day."

"It was an ordinary day," he said. "No major break-throughs, just pick and shovel work. I'm typing up the summary of my research to give to the tenure committee. How about you?"

"My day was not at all ordinary," Lisa said. "Someone tried to kill me."

Sam's face registered horror. It certainly seemed to be genuine horror. "What!" he exclaimed. "Why didn't you tell me?"

"I'm telling you. I was out running at about six this morning. A car came up behind me, headed straight for me. If I hadn't been next to some rocks and just barely had time to throw myself over them, I'd be mincemeat right now." She sipped, watched him.

His eyes held hers with intensity. "Were you hurt?"

"Only a little. I'll survive. Unless they try again."

"Did you go to the police?"

"Two cities' worth. No one seems to take this very seriously."

"What do you mean?"

"They think it was some macho motorist out to clear the roads of runners."

"You don't think so?"

"It was meant for me. Because I've been nosing into the Silverman-Hammer case."

"Stay out of it," Sam said. "I mean it. You're not going to find the murderer, if there is one, on your own. I'm worried about you."

Lisa looked at him, fingering her wineglass. Why wasn't he telling her about Dove going to his apartment? Why had he said nothing about the girl, acted as if he didn't know her? Lisa took another sip of champagne, staring at him steadily. He hadn't even told her he'd been at Page until she asked him about it. And she knew that if she hadn't asked him, he never would have told her. Just as he hadn't told her he knew Dove.

She said, "Last week when I tried to talk to Dove Kent about Silverman's murder, she seemed really upset, hysterical. Especially when I told her I wasn't sure it was Hammer who killed Silverman and then himself."

"So you think she might have tried to run you down?" Sam asked. He was ripping a cocktail napkin to shreds.

"Doesn't it sound like a possibility?" she asked. She could ask him about his meeting with Dove, but if she did, he could always come up with an explanation and she wouldn't know whether to believe it or not. It would be so much better if he would just bring it up himself. But he didn't. He continued to rip the napkin, making neat little piles of pieces on the edge of the coffee table.

"Yes," he said finally. "I think it's a possibility."

Lisa was silent, hoping now Sam would bring up Dove's visit. He didn't. She sighed and asked, "When is your preliminary tenure hearing?"

"Tuesday."

"And how are the experiments going?"

"We're close. I don't know if my projected conclusions will convince the committee that we're close to understanding the genetic patterns of adaptation of these viruses. If only I had another few months."

Lisa nodded. She'd heard this so often lately.

"You're not going to jog again tomorrow morning, are you?" he asked.

"I don't know. I haven't decided yet."

"Don't be a fool, Lisa," he said almost angrily.

"Then you believe it wasn't just a fluke?"

He scowled. "How do I know? I don't want you to find out by trying it again."

They were both quiet during dinner. The poached salmon and cucumber sauce seemed tasteless to Lisa. Afterward they did the dishes together. Sam said he was tired and would go home early. Lisa didn't try to detain him, didn't ask him any more questions. She felt only relief that he didn't want to stay, didn't want to make love to her. At her front door he kissed her quickly. His lips were dry and cool, and the impersonality of his kiss chilled her.

When he was gone, she sat on the sofa, looking over the Charles River to the lights of Boston beyond. Of course she wouldn't go jogging in the morning. She wasn't crazy. She could still feel the terror of that early-morning chase. The throbbing in her foot didn't let her forget. But where do I go from here? she asked herself. Clearly, Sam knew more than he was telling her. But what?

She thought of calling Brad to ask his advice. But she

didn't. She dialed Mary's number but hung up when she got Mary's answering machine.

When the doorbell rang and she heard Brad's voice on the intercom, she felt a wave of relief. "I was thinking about you," he said, "and I thought, if I came by, maybe you'd let me in."

If he had said something arrogant or brash, she would have told him off. Instead, she realized how much she wanted to talk to him. She pressed the buzzer and patted her hair down while waiting for him to climb the stairs.

When he was standing there beside her, she thought about how much she liked his looks. He was good-looking but not perfect, with a beaky nose and wide jaw. He was wearing chinos and a black crew sweater.

They were shy with each other as they sat on the sofa with glasses of brandy.

Brad noticed her ankle right away. "What happened?"

When she told him, his first reaction was alarm. "Somebody's after you."

Then she told him what the police thought. "Maybe. Maybe," he said, but he didn't sound convinced.

He seemed concerned when she told him about her discovery that Sam had been at Page when the science center was bombed. "And he didn't tell you?" he asked, surprised.

She shook her head. "Oh, he admitted it when I asked him."

They were silent. Finally Brad asked, "You really in love with him?"

Lisa was thoughtful. She said, thinking it out for the first time, "I thought I wanted to be. Now I'm not so sure I want to be." Then she rushed on with the rest of the story: how she had followed Dove and witnessed her meeting with Sam and how Sam had not mentioned one word about it.

"That is odd," Brad agreed. "Look, do you want me to check up on him?"

"How would you do that?"

"Oh, we have contacts with police, with private investigators. I could do some discreet checking. May take a few days. Just hold off until then. Okay?"

Lisa nodded. "I'd appreciate it," she said, sad that she could be so distrustful of Sam. "Meanwhile, I'll corner Dove, see if I can squeeze some information out of her."

Lisa sipped her brandy. She felt relieved already, just sharing her concerns with Brad. She felt very grateful to him. "Thanks," she said.

He had moved closer to her. "I've missed you, Lisa," he began, his voice husky. "I've missed you so much. At first I couldn't believe it when you broke it off. Then I was angry. I told myself you were a bitch, that you didn't care about me at all."

"It all seemed hopeless," she said. "We didn't seem to agree about anything."

"But we do," Brad said. "We agree about lots of things. And look how good an investigative team we are. What a shame Hennessy didn't hire you. We could've been magic together. We could crack this case."

She looked at him, hope growing like a balloon inside her chest.

He took her hand. She leaned toward him. Their kiss was like a small electrical shock, painful in its intensity. They kissed again and again.

"I remembered good, I forgot *how* good," he said.

Lisa was remembering, too. Her desire for Brad. It was so strong, it must mean something about his rightness for her.

Easily, as if they had never stopped doing so, they walked

into Lisa's bedroom hand and hand and removed each other's clothing with care. There was no time for play or sweet words. They came together like a thunderclap, as if their coupling were an inevitable natural phenomenon.

Spent, she lay beside him.

"I told you," he said. "We're good together. I've thought about you so often, missed you."

"I've missed you, too," she said.

"So why can't we start it up? Be the way we were at the beginning, the way we are right now. So it doesn't lose its spark."

Something was wrong. He wasn't saying what he was supposed to be saying. "Do you know what you're saying?"

He went right on, not noticing her anger, "I've given this a lot of thought. I love you, Lisa. But what I learned about myself is that I can't function in a really intense situation. You and I are a good team—and I don't mean just in bed. I think our trouble before was that we hadn't laid out the rules. We can do that. Like two grown-up people."

Shivering with rage, Lisa sat up. "Grown-up people," she croaked in a strange, strangled voice. "How can we act like grown-up people when you're a two-year-old." Grabbing her robe from the chair by the bed, she fled toward the bathroom. "Sam may be too old for me, as you say, but you, you have the body of a man and the mind of a child. Get out!"

"My God, Lisa, what the hell is the matter with you?"

She slammed the bathroom door and leaned against it. She could hear him muttering to himself in the bedroom. "Crazy. A crazy lady."

"And don't check up on Sam," she shouted. "I'm ashamed I agreed to it. You're not anywhere near the man Sam is. And you never will be. Get out of here!"

She heard nothing for a few moments except her own ragged breath. She tried to breathe slowly, deeply, to get control of herself. In a few moments she heard his angry voice right outside the bathroom door. "Another thing I guess I forgot is what a possessive nut you are. June at least understands me. Good-bye."

Lisa had herself well enough under control by now to be aware that instead of leaving he was waiting for her final words. She gave them to him. "I'm not sorry this happened. I've purged myself of you at last." And she knew that what she said was true.

She heard his heavy steps, the opening and slamming of the door, and Brad was out of the apartment and out of her life.

Under the punishing hot shower, Lisa remembered that it was Mary who had advised her to follow her heart. Lousy advice, but maybe it was lousy only because she didn't know the difference between her heart and her libido. This was one story she didn't think she would share with Mary.

CHAPTER 22

Tuesday, May 1, 1984

After a restless night during which the ache in her ankle was an insistent presence, Lisa overslept.

She slipped into Fletcher's lecture at 10:20 and took a seat in the back row. Fletcher was as boring as ever. As he droned on, Lisa searched the large lecture hall for Dove. Today she would stop her and *make* her explain some of these mysteries—her true feelings about Silverman, and now the added mystery of her meeting with Sam yesterday. This time she would nab her right after class, take her to that little French café on Main Street, ply her with croissants.

Lisa sighed. Food would mean nothing to a girl like Dove. How to make her talk? Lisa thought over possible strategies while trying to locate her in the lecture hall, which was about half as full as it had been for Fletcher's first lecture last Thursday. The man's big chance was fizzling fast. Lisa could just see those all-important student evaluations that could mean the end of an aspiring professor's hopes: "not that well prepared," "not as funny as Professor Silverman," "boring." She checked all of Dove's usual spots, but couldn't find her.

After class Lisa stopped by Mary's office. The note on the

door told her what she knew but had forgotten. Mary was at a meeting of Joycean scholars at the Hotel Commander in Cambridge. She'd be back at Addison tomorrow. Students requesting appointments to discuss their paper subjects should sign below with telephone numbers.

Lisa stopped at the phone outside the English Office and dialed Mary's number on the off-chance that she might not have gone to the morning meetings. Lisa knew Mary was on a panel in the afternoon called "The Many Faces of Leopold Bloom in *Ulysses*." She heard the mechanical click and the buzzing sound that meant Mary's answering machine was in operation. Her friend's optimistic voice edged with wry humor began, "Mary Reardon here. Or rather, I am not here at the moment. Please leave your name and telephone number, especially if you are a student with a paper problem, when you hear the beep."

Lisa smiled at the way Mary pronounced "beep." She enunciated it as if to *make* it a proper word by sheer force of will.

At the sound of the beep, Lisa said, "Hi, Mary, this is Molly Bloom. Can't find Leopold anywhere. Is he with you— or, at least, one of his many faces? Seriously, I want to talk to you. Please call me as soon as you can." Mary would know her voice. No problem there. They knew so much about each other. Lisa was eager to hear if Mary had had a chance to speak to Dove yet.

The rest of the morning Lisa had office hours. More students showed up than usual. They were worried about the hour exam scheduled for next Thursday. As one boy said, "We had Silverman psyched out. We knew what we had to deal with there. But Fletcher could ask anything."

On impulse, Lisa dropped in at Sam's lab at lunchtime. His lab assistant, a grad student whose brown beard looked like an imitation of Sam's, told her that Sam had called in sick. But when she telephoned his apartment there was no answer. A knot of anxiety began to form in the back of her mind. She tried to push it away.

Dove did not show up for Lisa's 4:00 writing seminar that afternoon, the first time she'd missed it.

At home Lisa called Lieutenant Cohen, then Lieutenant Gibson, to ask if they had discovered anything about her assailant. Both were busy and harassed. Both brushed her off and said they'd call if they had any news. She called Sam's apartment and let the telephone ring a dozen times before she hung up. The knot of anxiety grew larger. Finally she settled into her sofa and tried to concentrate on correcting student papers.

When the telephone rang at 5:30, Lisa leapt up eagerly. But it was only her mother, Anxious Anna, to ask how her ankle was. She had told her mother about the accident, but not about her suspicions that it wasn't an accident. Now she tried to sound cheerful and casual, but Anna could smell trouble, like a hound sniffing out pot.

"What's the matter? Is something wrong between you and Sam?" she asked.

Anna had predicted gloom and doom as the outcome of Lisa's relationship with Sam right from the start. She had certain criteria for Lisa's boyfriends. Anyone over forty didn't qualify. He must be young, professional. Good-looking was nice, but not a necessity, she had often told her daughter. In fact, too good-looking was not good. Absent Abe had been too good-looking. And that, probably, had been the cause of his leaving them. Too good-looking meant spoiled, women giving them the kind of look that made them dissatisfied with what they had. Anna would shake her head disapprovingly. Lisa didn't remember her father that way. Of course, after he left them, she had seen him only once and that was when he was dying, a bone-thin man with yellowed skin. She always remembered that final visit with a mixture of horror and guilt.

The telephone rang again at 6:30 as she was taking a yogurt from the refrigerator and thinking with grim satisfaction that at least the kind of anxiety she was feeling acted as a curb on her appetite. With her, it could easily go the other way. She remembered back to Mickey, her boyfriend before Brad. When he left her, she'd gone on an eating jag. She'd gained twenty pounds that winter. It had not been easy getting it off. She hated being a slave to her body's whims, yet one way or another she always seemed to be.

With the first ring of the telephone, she dropped the yogurt on the counter and raced to answer. The voice was female, unfamiliar, a kind voice, gentle and slow. "Jean Sullivan," the voice repeated. "I'm a nurse at Braeton General Hospital. A patient here named L. Dove Kent is asking for you. She's very upset. We're hoping that talking to you might calm her down. Could you come?"

"Dove!" Lisa exclaimed. "Why is she there? What happened?"

"An accident. On her bicycle. A car hit her," the sympathetic voice explained.

"Will she be all right?"

"We're hoping she will be," Jean Sullivan said in that kind voice. No promises.

Lisa had her hand on the doorknob when it suddenly occurred to her that she should accept nothing at face value. Even that kindly voice. After all, someone had tried to kill her yesterday morning. She found the number for Braeton General Hospital in the telephone book and called. To the high voice that answered "Braeton General" like a song, she asked, "Do you have a patient named L. Dove Kent?"

"Just a moment," the voice sang. "Yes, we do." "Do" was two syllables, a high note, then a lower one.

"Do you have a nurse named Jean Sullivan?"

"Yes, we do." No pause. Same melody.

Lisa looked nervously around the parking lot as she hurried to her car. It was dusk. People were arriving home from work. A few of them smiled and nodded to her, but she hardly noticed. She got into her car and forged into the stream of rush-hour traffic toward Braeton.

Questions tumbled about in Lisa's mind as she drove. How seriously had Dove been injured? Had it really been an accident? A strange coincidence, that Dove should be hit by a car the day after Lisa herself had had her narrow escape. If not an accident, if a deliberate hit-and-run, had the same person tried to kill both Dove and herself? And why did Dove insist on seeing her? Did she have something to confess? Or perhaps some secret knowledge to share, something that concerned Sam, something about her meeting with him yesterday afternoon? Or was it only that the poor child had no one to call to her bedside, no relatives, no friends, only Lisa, her teacher, whom she hardly knew at all?

Braeton General Hospital was a modern glass-and-concrete structure that spread out low to the ground in several wings. Lisa had passed it many times and hardly noticed it. Now she hurried inside through the glass doors and straight up to the front desk. "May I help you?" the receptionist sang in a voice that identified her instantly.

"I'm here to see Dove Kent, L. Dove Kent."

"I'm afraid she's not allowed to have visitors."

"Jean Sullivan called me a little while ago and asked me to come," Lisa explained.

The receptionist, a thin, dark-haired young woman, turned to a pile of index cards, thumbed through them, and picked one out, scrutinizing it carefully. "Yes," she said finally. "Dr. Muzzi has okayed it. You may go in."

"Where?"

The young woman pointed out the way, down a corridor to the right. "A-103."

Lisa pushed through a set of swinging doors and into a brightly painted yellow corridor with yellow tiles underfoot. She saw into rooms through half-opened doors. The assured staccato voices of TV news anchormen mixed with moans and conversation. Smells of alcohol and coffee and something sour made her stomach turn slightly.

The door to A-103 was nearly closed. She poked it open a little and saw a restless mound on the bed in the dimly lit room. Lisa went to the nurses' station a little farther down the hall. Several people were writing in notebooks, talking. One tired-looking young man in a green surgical gown with a mask hanging around his neck sat sipping coffee, his feet up on a chair.

Lisa cleared her throat, but no one paid any attention to her. "I'm looking for Jean Sullivan," she said.

A short, very pretty woman stood up, leaving her coffee on the desk. "Hi. I'm Jean," she said.

Lisa warmed to her immediately. She had the kind of smile that welcomed you, a wide grin, revealing a mouthful of large teeth. "You called me. I'm Lisa Davis."

Jean led the way back to Dove's room.

"Is she in pain?" Lisa asked.

"She's had some sedation," Jean answered. "That helps the

pain. We'd like to give her more, but she insists on talking to you."

Lisa stopped her at the door. "She'll be all right?" she asked.

"She's had a concussion, and her leg is broken. But she's looking better all the time," Jean said. "She's very upset about something. And Dr. Muzzi thought that if we did what she asked, sent for you, maybe she'd settle down. We called her aunt in Pittsburgh—her only relative—but she's unable to come. She also asked for Professor Reardon. She wasn't in. I left a message on her machine."

Jean opened the door. The mound moaned and thrashed on the bed. Jean switched on an overhead fluorescent light next to a small shiny sink in the corner and the room sprang into view, a box dominated by the hospital bed on which lay a figure swathed in bandages, leg encased in plaster and elevated on folded blankets. Jean plumped pillows and adjusted the slope of the bed behind Dove's head.

Lisa moved closer and could see Dove's face beneath a crown of bandages.

"Okay, my dear," Jean said, "here's your visitor as promised. Now you two have your little talk and then we'll get you that shot of Demerol. Give you a chance to start healing without all this jumping around." As she talked, she walked around Dove's bed straightening the bedclothes, helping the girl rearrange her bruised limbs.

Lisa felt tears of pity start up as she watched the girl on the bed, not much more than a child, and thought about some of the circumstances of her life. Jean placed a paper cup full of water with a plastic straw in front of Dove's lips. Dove's pale blue eyes, old with pain, met Lisa's over the straw as the girl sipped slowly.

When Dove finished drinking and spoke, it was not the voice that Lisa remembered. Halfway between a whisper and a groan, it wrenched at Lisa's heart. "Please wait outside, Jean."

The nurse looked dubious, but Dove insisted. "Please. This won't take long, and when it's over, I'll do whatever you say."

Lisa pulled a chair up to the bed. Dove's hand lay on the sheet. On impulse, Lisa covered it with her own. It was cold. Lisa rubbed it gently. "You're going to be all right," she said hopefully.

Dove was silent for a few moments, licking her lips. Her lips were pale, too. Her face, what showed beneath the bandage, was swollen and discolored. It pained Lisa to look at the girl's tired, watery eyes. Dove said something in such a low whisper that Lisa couldn't hear.

"What?" Lisa asked, bending closer.

"My father's journal," Dove said, barely audibly.

"Your father's journal," Lisa repeated encouragingly. "Your father kept a journal?"

Dove nodded, licked her lips again.

Lisa held the straw to Dove's lips as the girl sipped. Then she smoothed the pillows beneath her head and waited for her to say more. "Journal is at my house under the sugar in the canister on the counter."

Lisa nodded, wondering why she had hidden it.

"Get the journal," Dove continued, her voice stronger now, commanding. "Get it and bring it here, to me. Will you do that?" She looked intently at Lisa. The expression in her eyes was desperate.

"Okay, okay, I will," Lisa said, placating. "But first, would you tell me something about your accident?"

Assured that Lisa would bring her the journal, Dove sank back on the pillows, waited for Lisa's questions.

"When did it happen?"

"This morning. I was on my way to Silverman's—Fletcher's—lecture. As soon as I got to the end of my road, I was hit."

"Did you see the car?" Lisa asked.

Dove shook her head slightly. The motion made her wince. She said, "No. I know I came out of the road fast. I didn't really look. Car hit me from behind, and I was thrown off my bike. I heard the car speeding away before I lost consciousness. I guess I lay there for hours before a hitchhiker passed by and heard me moaning. If it wasn't for him . . ." she trailed off.

Lisa looked at the injured girl. She had closed her eyes and was lying very still. Lisa said, "The same thing happened to me when I was running yesterday morning—almost, only I managed to jump over a rock barrier and just missed getting hit."

"You mean you think it was deliberate?" Dove asked.

"Yes," Lisa replied. "I think someone wanted us out of the way."

"Why would someone want us out of the way?"

"I don't know. Did the police talk to you?"

Dove sighed. Put a hand to her head gingerly. "Yes. Some traffic patrolman came. Asked a lot of questions." Dove licked her lips again, and Lisa held the glass of water for her.

Lisa waited for Dove to say more. When she didn't, Lisa said, "Tell me about this journal of your father's."

Dove took a trembling breath and began, "My father always kept a journal. My mother told me so. And when Danny Connors was on trial for murder he thought my father's journal could help him. His lawyers searched the house then. Couldn't find it. No one could. It wasn't 'til last year—fifteen years later—I found it."

"Where was it?"

"He'd hidden it. In a box of his college chemistry books. No one ever thought of looking there. But last fall, when I started thinking about college, I sort of looked through his stuff. Finding his journal was—I don't know—like he wanted me to find it. And find it then. Like it was a message. I read it. Even though it hurt. It hurt and it made me feel closer to him than I ever had before. After I read it, I knew I had to come here, to Addison. It was like I knew what he wanted me to do."

Dove lay back on the pillows.

Jean opened the door and look in. "How ya doin'? She okay?"

"She's okay. We'll be through in five minutes."

Jean glanced at her patient and left, closing the door again. "You okay, Dove?"

Dove nodded.

"What did you think your father wanted you to do?" Lisa could see a pulse fluttering in Dove's white neck. What had this poor child believed her father wanted her to do? Avenge his death by murdering those who were responsible for it? But Hammer had not been responsible for Kent's death; he had come into the picture after Jim Kent was already dead, saved Silverman's skin. Would that be enough reason for Dove to avenge her father's death on Hammer as well as Silverman? Wait a minute, Lisa warned herself, if Dove were the one who had killed Silverman and then Hammer, why was someone now trying to kill her?

Dove was speaking, in her voice a new energy. "What he

wanted was for me to clear his name," she said, and with those words, her breath seemed to come more easily.

Lisa herself breathed a sigh of relief. Clear his name. The words sang, like the first birds of spring, in her head. Clearing Kent's name was a far cry from murdering two people to avenge his death. "But how," she asked, "how could you clear his name now? More than fifteen years later?"

Dove was silent for several moments. She turned her face toward the wall. She seemed to be struggling with herself about something.

"How?" Lisa pressed.

Dove turned her head back slowly. Her eyes were brimming with tears. "It was going to be a big secret," she began. "I was going to work it all out, by myself, and present it to the world. Then everyone would know. Everyone would know about . . ."—her words caught on a little sob—". . . about my father—the truth. It would be the truth."

"What would be?" Lisa asked gently.

"His story. The true story of the life—and death—of James Lincoln Kent. The story I'm writing."

"You've been writing his biography," Lisa said softly, understanding at last.

"His true biography. Taken from his journal. And from people who knew him. People who had really known him."

"Like Professor Sheldon Silverman," Lisa said, feeling a sudden lifting in her chest.

"Like Sheldon Silverman," Dove said bitterly.

"And that's why you came to Addison in the first place— to approach Silverman about your father."

"Yes. I knew he was here. I've followed his career."

"And Professor Louis Hammer?"

"Hammer, too."

Suddenly a big piece of the puzzle fit into place. "Sam Harrison," Lisa said. "He was at Page, too."

"Yes. But I didn't know that until about a month ago, until I realized he was the Sam Harrison my father had mentioned in his journal. Then I started calling him, trying to get him to talk to me, but he kept putting me off. Finally, yesterday, I talked to him."

"Why didn't he want to talk to you?" Lisa asked.

"On the phone he said he'd hardly known my father and could tell me nothing, but I bugged him until he agreed to see me."

"And when you saw him, was he able to tell you anything?"

"He told me nothing."

"Nothing at all?" Lisa probed.

"I asked him to tell me anything he could remember about my father, anything at all. I figured he'd have something to say, some opinion. After all, he was there."

"And he didn't?"

"He said he didn't know him. And that any opinion he gave about my father and the bombing wouldn't give me any comfort."

That sounds like Sam, all right, Lisa thought. He would do everything he could to avoid saying anything unkind to Dove about her father. Lisa began to smile to herself, but then a thought ripped into her: Why didn't Sam mention his meeting with Dove to her? She was talking to him about Dove last night, wondering whether Dove could have been the one who tried to run her down. She had given him every opportunity to tell her that Dove had been to his apartment that afternoon. She had even asked him what he had done all day. And he had not mentioned Dove's coming to see him. He had deliberately not mentioned it.

Lisa heard footsteps passing in the corridor. Any minute now Jean Sullivan would come back in and insist she leave her patient to get some rest. She'd better work fast if she wanted to find out more. She began eagerly. "So you talked to Professor Silverman about your father," imagining with what panic Silverman must have reacted to Dove's appearance on the Addison campus, a threat to everything he'd lied and cheated and paid Hammer off for. "Did you tell him about finding your father's journal?"

"Oh, no," Dove said. "I knew how threatening that would be to him. If he knew about the journal, he'd stop at nothing until he got his hands on it. You see, my father's journal proves that Silverman was involved in the bombing of Lohr Science Center. If the police had found it after the bombing, Silverman would've been tried along with Danny Connors."

"So what did you want from him, if not an admission of his guilt? What did you think he could tell you about your father?"

"They were in lots of organizations together—SDS, Students for a Non-Violent World, Campus Anti–Vietnam War Coalition, and others. According to my father's journal, they'd talked way into the night, he and Silverman and Danny Connors. I thought he could tell me about my father's beliefs, how he expressed them, things like that."

"And did he?" Lisa asked, knowing the answer.

"He said he hadn't known him. He practically shoved me out of his office."

If Silverman had carried out his assigned role in the bombing, Dove's father would be alive today. "No wonder you hated him," Lisa said aloud.

Dove looked directly at Lisa, very alert now. "I hated him with everything in me. I looked at his selfish face and I wanted to squash him like the worm he was. But one thing I've learned all these years growing up without having anything I wanted, I've learned that you must decide exactly what you want, then go after it. You don't worry about how you feel. You just think about getting what you want."

Lisa nodded.

Dove continued, "My father's biography would have told the truth about Silverman. I would've gotten even. I would've proven his guilt. And that's just what I'll do even though Silverman's dead now and can't be punished by it. I'll show the world who my father was, who he really was." Now Dove lay still, breathing deeply, her eyes shining with purpose.

Lisa sat lost in thought for a few moments, then asked, "Why would someone want to kill you? And me?"

"Maybe we know too much," Dove said simply.

"But what?" Lisa thought for a moment. "I've been going around telling people that I have reason to believe the killings were not murder-suicide. But you haven't done that. You told me you believed in the murder-suicide theory."

"But I've been asking questions about my father, stirring it all up again. Maybe someone is afraid I know something."

"But who? Silverman and Hammer are both dead. Who else would be threatened by something you might know?"

"I don't know. Someone thinks I know something. But what? I was only two years old when it happened. What could I know? And who could feel threatened by what I know?" She coughed. Lisa brought the straw to Dove's lips.

When she had put the glass back on the bedside table, Lisa said, "Maybe someone thinks you know something because of your father's journal . . ."

"But I haven't told anyone that I found it. Except . . ." She stopped, her eyes opening wide.

"Who did you tell?"

"Professor Harrison. Yesterday."

Lisa felt a strange thudding in her chest. She had to wait a moment before she could speak. "You told Sam Harrison? Why?"

Dove didn't answer. She was crying silently, tears slipping from the outer corners of her eyes.

Lisa sat forward and held her hand again. "What is it, Dove?" she asked, overwhelmed with sympathy.

"I didn't want to tell him about the journal. I didn't want anyone to know about it. When I talked to him on the phone, at first he said he didn't know anything about it, didn't remember my father at all. A few days ago I called and told him that my father had written about him in his journal. That interested him, all right. He wanted to know what my father had said about him. Seemed to upset him. I told him that we had to talk in person. That's when he agreed to see me."

Lisa was silent as she remembered the tears streaming down Dove's cheeks as she rode away from Sam's apartment yesterday afternoon, and a new image of Sam began to form in her mind. He had been unsympathetic to Dove, perhaps even cruel. "And what had your father written about Professor Harrison in his journal?" she asked.

"Something about how he and Danny Connors were worried about Professor Harrison's experiment being destroyed in the bombing. To tell you the truth, I skimmed that part. It didn't really interest me. Now I'd like to read it more carefully."

"Dove, I think we should tell the police about the journal. Let them get it. See what they think of it."

Dove's tears were flowing steadily now. "I don't want them to have it," she sobbed. "It's mine. Mine. My father left it for me. I have to do what he wanted me to. If the police get it, and the newspapers, who knows what kind of awful things they'll say about my father?"

"Okay, okay," Lisa soothed.

"Promise?"

"Promise." She would do what Dove asked now. Later she would try to convince the girl to show it to the police.

Dove reached out and took Lisa's hand. It was a first. Lisa sat quietly next to her. Dove held on, her eyes closed, lids fluttering, until Jean Sullivan returned.

The nurse smiled when she saw her patient had quieted down and was ready to sleep.

"The key is in the drawer," Dove said calmly as Jean readied her for the shot.

Lisa slipped out, Dove's housekey in hand, feeling more than a little afraid of what she had promised to do.

CHAPTER 23

Lisa felt a shiver of fear as she drove. It was a black night with only a few stars and a slice of a moon. The darkness was punctuated occasionally by the lights of farmhouses beside the road, spaced so far apart that each friendly winking cluster came as a surprise.

It was foolish to come out here alone, Lisa was thinking as she cranked the window open and breathed in clean night air. She should have called the Braeton police. She should have tried to reach Lieutenant Cohen and told him about James Kent's journal. But she'd promised Dove. At least she should have called Mary and left a message if she wasn't there. As for Brad, she was through with him. And she certainly couldn't have asked Sam for help. Not now. Sam was keeping too many secrets from her. She no longer trusted him. Can you love someone you don't trust? She thought of the night he'd asked her to marry him. In his bed, his warm, strong arms around her.

Lisa sighed. The countryside had been totally dark for some time now. Either there were no houses here or their occupants were asleep in their beds, comfortable and safe. She was approaching the railroad crossing. The next dirt road to the left after the crossing was Dove's road.

Lisa drove beyond Dove's turnoff to the place by the side of the road hidden by trees where she had waited for Dove yesterday. Was it only yesterday? It seemed like a lifetime ago. She parked and walked along the highway back to Dove's road. As she turned onto the bumpy dirt road, she thought she saw a momentary flash of light through the trees.

Lisa didn't see the light again. Perhaps it was only moonlight reflected from one of the reflectors placed on trees nearest the road. For when she rounded a bend and came upon the low Cape Code house set in the pine grove, it was dark and silent. Not a bicycle or a car in sight. Only the house nestled in pines, a dark silhouette against a gray-black sky. The windowpanes glittered like black ice in the dim light of the moon. Tall evergreens, hulking monsters, pressed on the little cape as if trying to reclaim their space.

Lisa started up the pine-needled path, but turned her head quickly as a sudden breeze made sighing sounds in the branches. The sight of the swaying branches calmed her. It's only the wind, she whispered to herself. She continued up the path, clutching Dove's key in her fist.

As she fumbled at the keyhole in the darkness, she wished she had brought a flashlight. If it were daylight with sun dappling through the trees and birds twittering in the branches, she would feel unafraid. But now in the dark, with the rustling and shadowing of trees and the watchful blackness all around, she was terrified. She couldn't wait to get inside and flood the little house with electric light. She could grab the journal out of the canister in the kitchen and get out of here. I should have called Lieutenant Cohen and insisted he accompany me, she told herself, as she pushed against the door. If

Dove's suspicions were correct, someone must be after the journal, someone who would stop at nothing to get it.

The door opened gently, easily inward. Lisa stepped over the threshold onto some kind of a rug. But she could see nothing. It was blacker inside than outside. Shades or curtains must be drawn over the windows. She inched along the wall, her hand sliding against a rough wooden surface as she searched for a light switch. Her leg slammed with a loud thwack into a hard shin-high object. "Ow," she yelled.

Even as she was shouting she heard a noise, a rustling, like someone shifting weight, and a blinding light was flashed into her eyes. Circles of light leaped startlingly before her, reds and whites and yellows, forming and dissolving.

"Lisa!" a familiar voice cried. "God. It's you." Sam. His voice husky with fear.

She heard his great exhalation of breath. Relief. Who had he expected it to be? And why the hell was he here? "Would you mind getting that light out of my eyes?" she asked, trying to control the trembling in her voice.

The light moved from her face to the floor. "Oh, I'm sorry," he said, relief still softening his voice. Whoever he was afraid of, it certainly wasn't her. But she *was* afraid. Her head throbbed with fear. Her cheeks burned. Her heart started up a funny, erratic dance of its own, like a motor in disrepair. She leaned against the wall for a moment, willing strength back into her body, grateful that her face must be as unknowable as his, lighted only by the flashlight beam dancing on the planked wooden floor.

"I didn't see your car," she gasped, the first words that came into her head.

"I parked behind the house."

Yes, of course, he'd hidden his car. Just as she had. Why

hadn't she thought of that? "What are you doing here?" she asked as evenly as she could manage.

His expression flickered with the light. "I'm looking for something," he said.

"What?" Lisa asked. Sam had the answer to the puzzle. He had only to say it and it would be over. To tell her he was looking for Jim Kent's journal and why.

"I can't tell you. Not yet. Trust me."

Lisa nodded, thinking, How could I ever have trusted you?

"Why are *you* here?" he asked, as if noticing for the first time the oddity of their unplanned meeting here in the dark of Dove's house.

"She asked me to come," Lisa said cautiously.

"Here. Hold this." He handed her the flashlight. She trained it on the desk as he carefully looked through the contents of the top drawer. The back of his neck, exposed, looked vulnerable. She could so easily hit him over the head with the heavy flashlight and make a run for it, she thought. But she didn't move. "That poor child," Sam said, still rifling through the desk. "You heard about her accident?"

For a moment Lisa was speechless with the shock of his knowing. Did he know about it because he'd been responsible for it? "How do you know about it?" she asked.

"I was in the English office looking for you late this afternoon when the call came in. From the hospital. They were trying to find a relative to notify."

Lisa wondered if there had been such a call. It would be easy to check. All she had to do was ask Edith Waks tomorrow. If tomorrow ever came, she thought morbidly. Wasn't that the name of a song—or something? Sam's head was bent over the bottom desk drawer now as his eager fingers scrabbled through its contents. Now. She could do it now.

She looked down at the gray ringlets framing a bald spot at the top of his head. She hadn't even known he had a bald spot. She'd never had this view of him before. The nape of his neck looked thin and white, the curls that straggled down there shaded into a darker color. Again the sense of his vulnerability blunted her purpose. She could never hit him, not this way. She wasn't sure, not yet, what this was all about, how he was involved, what he had done. Anyway, it was too late. He was standing up.

"Why did you say Dove wanted you to come?" he asked as he straightened up, rubbing the small of his back.

Lisa thought quickly. "To bring her some clothes."

Sam asked with apparent concern, "How is she?"

"They say she'll be okay."

Sam took the flashlight.

"Why don't we just turn on the light?" Lisa asked. She couldn't stop herself from shuddering, a spasm that shook her whole body. If Sam were responsible for the murders and the attempted murders, why did he want the lights off? Who was there to be afraid of now? Dove was safely hospitalized, out of the way. She was already here, supposedly unsuspecting and at his mercy.

"I don't want anyone to surprise us," Sam answered.

Maybe it was the police he was worried about. "Can I help you look for whatever it is you're looking for?" Lisa asked.

Sam ran his fingers through his rumpled curls. In the reflected flashlight beam, his face looked gray. Old, collapsed. Wrinkles, jowls emphasized in shadow, eyes washed out, no color. Lisa couldn't read them. "Oh, thanks, Lisa," he said as if he really appreciated her offer to help, "but I have to do this myself. I would like it if you'd hold the flashlight for me again, though."

If she didn't know better, she'd be sure he was the same old Sam, kind, grateful for her attention. But who *was* the same old Sam? Had he ever been someone she knew? Or only an illusion created out of her need for him?

Sam was on his knees searching through cabinets built in under bookshelves along one wall of the living room. Full of records neatly arranged on racks, the cabinets yielded no secrets. Most of the articles in the house belonged to the mathematics professor who was on sabbatical. Dove had told Lisa, at one of their first meetings, how lucky she was to get this place so that she didn't have to live in a dorm. She took care of his plants and kept the place clean; in return, she paid no rent.

Sam was struggling to his feet. "I've checked everywhere but the kitchen," he said. "Come. It's this way." He took her arm, guiding her as she aimed the flashlight on the floor ahead of them.

The kitchen was a large room with deep soapstone sinks in one corner and an old black stove on delicate legs. Next to the sinks was a butcher block counter and underneath it a row of cabinets. Sam opened those and Lisa trained the light on the shelves which, unlike the living room cabinets, were messy, with cans of food and cereal boxes leaning against one another tipsily. On the bottom shelf was an assortment of much-used pots and pans.

Sam clattered about among the pots, knocked over a stack of cans. "Dammit," he muttered. "Here. Let me have the flashlight." He poked and pried, shining the light in corners, into pots.

Lisa watched him, feeling goosebumps start on the backs of her arms. Sam had an old black car. She hadn't checked it for scrapes, hadn't even thought of it. Maybe she'd never have the chance now. Should I just make a dash for it? she wondered. She pictured herself racing through the dark house, out across the front yard, down the pitch-black dirt road to her car. She could run faster than he could, she was sure. She'd jump in, lock the doors, start up, and drive straight to the Braeton police. She'd tell them . . . What? What would she tell them? What did she suspect Sam of, anyway? Of murdering Silverman and Hammer? Of trying to run her down? Of hitting Dove while she was bicycling? Who would believe such a bizarre story? Did she believe it herself?

Sam was getting up from the cabinets. The flashlight shone on several undisturbed glass canisters on the counter next to the stove. The canisters didn't seem to tempt Sam at all. He was resting his elbow on the counter, practically looking right at them. The largest one held flour halfway up the jar, which looked like a huge mayonnaise jar. The jar next to it was filled almost to the top with what appeared to be sugar. Sam let the beam drop to the floor. He was looking dissatisfied, the way he did when an experiment wasn't turning out the way he hoped.

"Can you tell me now?" she asked. If only he would give her some simple explanation for being here, then she could relax, they could laugh about it, this whole nightmare would be over.

They heard the sound of tires outside. Sam turned the flashlight off. "Dammit. The police," he muttered. With his words, Lisa felt everything crashing down around her. The nightmare was real; Sam was some kind of a monster. His hold on her arm as he pushed her back with him against the wall seemed viselike, menacing. "Be quiet," he whispered.

Outside a car door slammed shut with no attempt at stealth. Above the sound of their own breathing, they heard footsteps crunch up the pine-needled path, then a knocking on the front door. A voice called out cheerfully, "Lisa! Lisa, darling. Where are you?"

Tearing herself away from Sam's grasp, Lisa ran toward the front door. "Mary. Mary, is that really you?" she called out, her voice edged with panic, as she pulled the door open. With the door open and a shaft of moonlight streaming in, Lisa found the light switch on the wall and turned it on, flooding the room with light.

Mary closed the door behind her and leaned against it. She was wearing her heathery tweed suit that picked up the red in her hair and made it look like a flaming bush on the heath. Her shoes were the shoes she'd bought in Dublin—real brogues, she called them—orange-red, the color of her hair, fringed with flaps of leather over the laces. She looks like an orange angel, Lisa thought as she looked at her gratefully.

"Dove told me you'd be here," Mary said.

"Mary, Sam is looking . . ."

"Hello, Mary," Sam said from directly behind Lisa. "What are you doing here?"

"I might ask you the very same," Mary said with a smile. "I stopped at the hospital to see Dove when I found the message on my answering machine that she wanted to see me. She told me that I would find Lisa here. But I didn't expect you, Sam. Did you come together?"

"No," Lisa answered quickly. "Dove asked me to come and pick up some of her clothes. I don't know why Sam is here." She said it pointedly. She tried to telegraph a message through her eyes to Mary: Sam is here uninvited. Be careful.

"What are you doing here?" Mary asked Sam with sudden suspicion. "Did you know Dove?"

"No. I mean, yes. I . . ." He stopped trying to explain himself and turned to Lisa. "Look, Lisa, why don't you and

Mary go ahead and get some of Dove's things together while I just look a bit more. Then I'll go home."

"Okay, Sam, okay," Lisa said as if she were talking to a madman or a child in the middle of a tantrum. "C'mon, Mary. Let's go upstairs and get Dove's clothes for her." She pulled at the tweedy suit jacket, feeling the roughness of fabric between her trembling fingers. As they climbed the stairs, they could hear Sam rummaging around in the kitchen again.

At the top of the narrow wooden staircase was the door to a little bedroom under the eaves. Lisa pulled Mary in and closed the door firmly behind them. The room was neat and smelled of cedar. Lisa sat on the bed wearily. Mary stood before her and asked, "What is going on here? You're acting as if Sam is Jack the Ripper."

"I'm worried," Lisa said in confusion. "He's acting very strangely."

"What do you mean, strangely?"

"Did Dove say anything to you about her father's journal?"

Mary shook her head. "I only saw her for a moment. She was doped up. She told me only that you were here. What's this about a journal?"

"Dove's father kept a journal. I guess it's got some pretty important stuff in it. She sent me here to get it."

"So that's what she meant," Mary said. "She said she wanted me to come here and help you. She didn't like the idea that you were here alone. Why didn't you call the police or someone to come with you?"

"Dove asked me not to," Lisa explained.

"I see," Mary said. "But what is Sam doing here?"

"I think he's looking for the journal. He doesn't know that I know about it. I think he's dangerous," she said almost in a whisper.

"What do you mean, dangerous?"

"He could be the killer. He must have had something to do with that bombing in 1968. He could've killed Silverman and Hammer because of it, whatever it was he was involved in. Maybe because they knew something. He might've been the one who tried to kill me when I was running yesterday morning because he thought I knew something, or was about to find out something about him. Then yesterday afternoon, Dove went to see him to ask him about her father. I think he tried to run her down this morning, just as he had me, because he feared she knew too much. She told him about the journal. There's something in that journal. Something he wants. And he'll stop at nothing to get it."

"Where is the journal?" Mary asked.

"In the sugar canister in the kitchen. Not such a great hiding place, but it seems to have worked so far."

"Let's try to head him off," Mary said.

"Maybe we should just get out of here," Lisa said nervously. But Mary was already opening the door softly, trying not to make a sound. Lisa grabbed a pillowcase off the bed.

"What's that for?" Mary asked.

"He'll get suspicious if we haven't gotten the clothes we supposedly came for," she whispered, as she stuffed some clothing into the pillowcase.

They tiptoed down the stairs. It was strangely quiet. The stairs were dark. Sam had turned out the lights. Mary took the lead. Swiftly but silently she glided through the front hall, through the living room, and into the kitchen.

Sam was hunched over the kitchen counter concentrating deeply on something in front of him. With one hand he held the beam of his flashlight steadily before him, with the other hand he held something Lisa couldn't see. Her eye went to the counter where the sugar canister had been. It was there still, tipped on its side next to a mound of sugar. She couldn't help a little horrified intake of breath. Involuntarily she began to move backward, toward the front door, toward safety. Now that Sam had found the journal, what would he do to Mary and her in order to prevent them from telling about it?

Lisa was surprised to see that Mary, instead of backing away, was edging forward as quiet as a cat slinking toward a sparrow. Mary turned toward her briefly and put a finger to her lips. Lisa watched as Mary picked up a bronze urn standing in the living room next to the kitchen entranceway. Lisa knew what Mary was about to do and she wanted to stop her. But something had to be done. Earlier, she had not been able to hit Sam over the head with his flashlight because the back of his neck seemed so vulnerable, because she wasn't sure of his guilt, because she had thought she loved him. Now Mary was going to do what she should have done herself. And she had all she could do not to reach out and grab the weapon from Mary's hand and shout out a warning to Sam. She stood absolutely still, hardly daring to breathe. Mary's arm went up, the edges of the urn shone with reflected light from Sam's flashlight beam.

Maybe it was the choked scream that involuntarily rose from her throat. Maybe it was the sound the urn made as it swished through the air. Or maybe it was just an instinctive intimation of danger. Whatever it was, Sam turned as the urn crashed down with force, hitting him a blow that glanced off his ear onto his shoulder.

"Ugh," he gasped. His hand came up quickly to the side of his head; the flashlight fell to the kitchen floor and shattered, its light extinguished. In the dark he turned and stumbled, facing Mary, who still held the urn. As Sam lifted his arm to strike at Mary, Lisa jumped forward, flailing the pillowcase full of Dove's clothes. She hit Sam in the face with it. And as Sam lost his balance, Mary was able to hit him again: swinging the urn like a baseball bat, she hit him on the side of the head full force. Sam toppled over without a sound.

Lisa screamed, ran to him, and cradled his head in her arms. "Oh, Sam, Sam," she crooned, sure he was dead, all his many kindnesses to her flooding over her.

Mary was beside her, bending over the unconscious man. She switched on the kitchen light and rummaged hurriedly through the pillowcase as Lisa examined Sam, who seemed to be sleeping peacefully. He was breathing rhythmically, she saw with relief. But an ugly welt on the side of his head was already swelling into a purplish lump.

"Here," Mary said, businesslike, "we'll tie him up."

"But Mary, he's hurt. Let's call an ambulance."

"He's not badly hurt," Mary reassured her. "I didn't hit him that hard. He's just out. But he could come to any minute and then we're in trouble."

When Lisa said nothing in agreement, Mary added convincingly, "He knows we're onto something. We won't be safe if he regains consciousness."

With mixed feelings, Lisa watched as Mary tied Sam's hands behind his back with one of Dove's blue kneesocks. When she'd finished, Mary got another sock and tied that around Sam's feet. "There," she said, standing back, "that ought to take care of him. I always knew my girl guide knots would come in handy someday."

The little book over which all this fuss had been made was on the floor under the counter where Sam had dropped it when he was hit. Lisa picked it up. It was a brown suede looseleaf notebook, now covered with a dusting of sugar.

Lisa opened it. It was filled with lined paper, both sides of which were covered with a dense, scrawly writing. Lisa read the first page:

September 9, 1967. These are exciting times. I feel privileged to be alive in a time when an awareness is beginning to sweep this country. There are so many causes to fight for. First: we must stop this war, end the exploitation of a small defenseless country in the name of the crusade against Communism. We must train a new generation with love instead of hatred. Already Stella and I are teaching our Little Dove to love, to . . .

The book was ripped from her hand. Mary stood over her. "What are you doing?" Mary asked. Lisa had never before seen such a look on the beautiful professor's face. Mary held the book tightly to her breast. Her mouth was hard. Her eyes blazed.

"What is it? What's the matter, Mary?" Lisa asked.

Mary's face seemed to dissolve. "I don't know. I feel as if I may faint. I've never struck anyone before. I guess I wanted you to help, to share the responsibility with me. And, instead, you were sitting here reading the journal. But I understand. You still can't accept the fact that he's a murderer. You don't want to."

Sam was moaning softly, turning from side to side, trying to free himself, still not awake. Lisa looked over at him, then said to Mary, "No, of course I don't want to. I'm still hoping it isn't so."

Mary was swaying. Lisa helped her to a chair, got out a glass from the cabinet, and poured her a glass of water. "Are you all right?" she asked.

Mary nodded, sipping water, still holding the journal to

her breast. "I'll just sit here for a minute, catch my breath. Then we'll decide what to do." Mary seemed uncertain.

Sam was struggling with his bonds now. The sight of him tied on the floor and of the swelling lump on his head made Lisa feel sick. Had she really loved this man? she asked herself. How could she love a murderer? She must find out the truth about him. Without another word, she hurried into the living room where she had noticed a telephone. The softly purring buzz on the line calmed her. She had just punched 911 when she felt a crashing pain on the side of her head over her left ear. There was an explosion of brilliant colors inside her head, a gigantic whirring sound, and then blackness, nothingness spread out all around her, enveloped her, like a dark, dark night. A brittle, sharp-edged nothingness. She fought it, flailing, and heard a cry, far away, that must be her own voice. And then nothing.

CHAPTER 24

At Braeton police headquarters Cohen sat by the telephone. He was waiting for a call that could answer all his questions. He was getting that prickly feeling in the back of his neck, the feeling he always got when he was coming close, very close, to the end. He'd been surprised when he got the report about Dove Kent's accident from Traffic this afternoon. Both Lisa Davis and the Kent girl victims of hit-and-run drivers in the past two days. Strange.

He looked up at the clock on the wall. 7:37. Eva had nearly cried when he'd called to tell her he'd be late again to-night. She had made her grandmother's recipe for pot roast. Cohen salivated at the thought of the succulent feast he was missing. Strange about those accidents, he thought. Still, accidents happened every day. In Cambridge the accident rate was zooming as the numbers of physical health nuts taking to the roads increased. Jencks had said so when he called to report on the paint scrapings on the rocks on Greenough Boulevard. The car had been a Chevy, at least ten years old, with a layer of black paint over the original maroon. Probably not many like it on the road. If it was a local car, the area traffic police might spot it sooner or later. The Kent girl's accident in Braeton had occurred on that rural stretch of Main Street, a two-lane road with sharp curves, one of the worst. Six accidents on that road in the past month. And Traffic told him the girl admitted coming out of the side road too fast. Still . . .

The Kent accident had started him thinking. Maybe, just maybe, he was beginning to see how some pieces of this puzzle might fit together.

Earlier this evening, when he was rereading the suicide note, he'd gotten some new ideas. He'd called up Hughes. Luckily, caught him just as he was leaving his apartment to pick up a date, and sent him out to follow up a hunch. Cohen's hunch had to do with the car, the old Chevy with a layer of black paint. If his hunch was right, Hughes should know something about the car by now. Cohen had alerted Jencks, called him at home, and told him there could be urgent business this evening. Jencks was sitting in front of his TV set waiting.

The telephone rang. Hughes, his voice high with excitement, calling from the two-way radio in his car. "Lieutenant, I found the Chevy. It's here, just where you thought it would be. I didn't even need to use the search warrant. No one's in the house. I went to the carriage house, just like you said, and I could see the car by shining my flashlight in through the window, once I rubbed some of the grime off. Then I found a window with a broken lock, eased it up, and let myself in. It's the car, all right, an old Chevy painted black. I called Jencks just like you said. He'll be right over."

Cohen wished he could go and see the car himself. But he was still waiting for a telephone call, the one that could mean the solution of this case.

CHAPTER 25

"It's all right. It's all right," a voice was crooning. A familiar voice.

Lisa tried to open her eyes. She was slumped in a chair in Dove's kitchen, her hands tied to the slats that made up the chair back, her ankles tied to the chair legs. The pain in her head was intense, and she was moaning. She'd been dreaming of murder, a dream she'd had before. She held a hammer in her hand. She had killed someone. Yet, it was she, herself, who was bleeding. The pain in her head throbbed steadily, like strokes of a hammer. She heard herself moaning again.

"It's all right, Lisa." Sam's voice was soft, low, yet trembling with an emotion she couldn't identify.

Lisa opened her eyes and realized with a jolt that it was not all right, not all right at all. And, certainly, Sam was in no position to tell her anything was all right. He was no longer trussed up on the floor as he had been when she raced for the telephone—how long ago? She had no idea. Time had stopped for her. Now Sam, too, was tied to a chair on the other side of the wooden kitchen table. But even tied up like that, helpless, he wanted to help her, to tell her everything was all right.

"What do you mean, all right?" she asked plaintively. Then, as if in surprise, she said, "My head hurts." The words came out in a whine. In an attempt to sound brave she asked briskly, "What happened?"

"It seems that our Mary is obsessed with hitting people over the head with that brass urn," Sam said with a weak smile.

"Mary! She hit me? But why?"

"Probably for the same reason she hit me," Sam said.

Lisa shook her head and then stopped because the shaking was too painful. "She hit you because she thought you were the murderer," she said, and even as she said it, she wondered when she had stopped believing that he might be. She had been convinced of his guilt. She had convinced Mary. Or so she had thought. Maybe Mary hadn't needed convincing. Oh, God. Her head was throbbing so much, she couldn't make any sense out of anything.

"How did she talk you into thinking I was the murderer?" Sam asked.

Lisa was fighting against the material that bound her hands behind her back. But to no avail. Mary had done her work well. Lisa's wrists seemed to be tied with another of Dove's kneesocks. With a sigh of frustration, she stopped battling and sat still, moving her fingers, trying to get the circulation back into her hands. "She didn't convince me, Sam. You did."

"I did?"

Lisa nodded wearily. Sam's face was all innocence. Wide eyes. Mouth slightly open. Who, me? Could she believe him? Maybe yes. Maybe no. But why the hell had Mary hit her and tied her up along with Sam? Either Mary thought Lisa was in cahoots with Sam or she wanted Lisa tied up and out of the way because—oh, no, it couldn't be Mary. It just couldn't be. Okay, she told herself, trying to breathe deeply, calmly, maybe Mary thought Lisa and Sam were the murderers. Maybe she was calling the police right now. But if Mary was calling the police, Lisa thought, she would hear her. No. She wasn't calling the police. Lisa heard a car door slam. Mary was outside doing something in her car. There must be some explanation for her strange behavior. Other than the obvious explanation—the one she didn't even want to think about.

"I don't understand," Sam was saying. "You thought I killed Silverman? And Hammer? Why would I do that?"

"You haven't been honest with me about a lot of things."

Sam's innocent expression was fading. "That's absurd," he said, but he looked away.

Lisa sighed. "I followed Dove yesterday when she went to your apartment. She stayed there for over twenty minutes, asked you questions about her father. She told me that today. Yet you never told me. And you were here hunting for Jim Kent's journal, but you wouldn't tell me what you were looking for."

"Okay. I didn't know you knew about the journal. I didn't want to tell you about it. I would have, though, when it was all over."

"When what was all over?" Mary asked in what seemed like a parody of her usual cheerful voice. She walked briskly back into the kitchen. She had put on a pair of old-fashioned ladies' black gloves and was carrying a small faded hand towel.

"What's this all about, Mary?" Lisa asked. "Why did you hit me, tie me up?" Lisa had some idea, a last hope really, that Mary had made a horrible mistake, had somehow connected her, along with Sam, to the murders.

Mary was wiping the urn with the towel. She stopped for a moment and looked over at Lisa. "You really don't understand, you poor dear, do you?" she asked in that wonderful, kind voice that Lisa had loved ever since she had met the red-haired Irish woman.

"Is this some kind of a hideous joke? What is it, Mary? We've been friends." Lisa couldn't help it; the last sentence came hopelessly from her lips.

"I suppose I owe you an explanation before you both go gentle into that good night," Mary said in her old sincere voice.

Lisa gasped, hope fading quickly as Mary made the reference to Dylan Thomas's poem about facing death. So they were to die. Both she and Sam.

Mary held up the journal and slapped it against her gloved hand. "You'll understand when I read you some of this," she said.

How could I have been so stupid, Lisa wondered. If only I hadn't thrown the pillowcase at Sam, he might have been able to defend himself in that crucial moment when Mary hit him with the urn. But I trusted Mary. We've been such good friends. Oh, if only I had called Lieutenant Cohen. I should never have come out here alone.

Mary was flipping pages. "Ah, here's something interesting," she said pleasantly. "It's going to work out quite well that the two of you are here. Listen and you'll understand." She began to read. " 'The plans for the bombing are moving, but Danny keeps bringing up Sam Harrison's experiment. He's really worried about its being ruined when we bomb Budlong's lab. Sam's lab is right next door. Danny said Sam's experiment is so good it could win him a Nobel, that Sam will be very, very angry if anything happens to that experiment. Shel explained it all away in that annoying holier-than-thou tone he gets when he's being The Great Revolutionary.' "

Mary closed the little book with a finger holding the place and smiled at Sam with everything but her eyes. "So, Sam, the experiment you had nearly completed in 1968 at Page University could have resulted in your being awarded a Nobel Prize, or so rumor had it at the time. But, instead, all your fine work was blown up." Mary raised her arm high in the air. "Boom," she shouted into the silence of the room.

Sam was squirming, trying to free himself.

"You must have been very, very angry at Sheldon Silverman, then a lowly graduate student, who blew up your experiment," Mary said.

"Wait a minute," Sam said. "I never even knew that Silverman was involved in the bombing. He was cleared by a grand jury."

"All right," Mary said easily. "You suspected he was involved. And your suspicions are confirmed here, in Kent's journal. So, you were angry at Silverman then and even angrier now, because you were never able to reproduce the experiment that was destroyed." Mary smiled as she continued, "The genius, or perhaps only the luck, that led to that nearly complete experiment in 1968 has eluded you, Professor Harrison. Ever since then, your career has moved relentlessly downward. Am I not right?

"And now you are coming up for tenure here at Addison and you want it desperately. This is your last chance. The last gasp, is that the American expression, Lisa? I wonder, my dear Sam, if it crossed your slightly overaged brain how much you would like to kill Professor Silverman when he was awarded the prestigious Finstermann Chair, his fortune, his future secure at this fine institution while you, who have worked much harder, much longer, and with so little success, could have succeeded, could have reached the greatest heights of modern science but for his wanton destruction of your experiment, along with a few lives."

Sam's face was red with fury. "You killed him. I didn't," he shouted. "Kill. My God, I even have trouble injecting my rats with germs."

Mary laughed her throaty laugh. "Of course you didn't kill him, Sam. Or Lou Hammer. As you say, you couldn't kill a rat. I said only that you would have liked to kill him, that you had motivation to kill him, not that you did it. I killed them, as you must realize by now."

"Why would you shoot Silverman?" Lisa asked. She shuddered as she thought of the brutality of the murder. "And Hammer? And you must have been the one who tried to run me down. And hurt Dove, tried to kill her. But why?"

Mary was smiling tolerantly, slapping the leather-bound book against the palm of one gloved hand. "Ah, my little Lisa, you are too good to be true. Not stupid. No, not at all stupid, but your mind runs so to goody-goody philosophy that the realities of life as we know it are rarely apparent to you. I wish I could teach you. But alas, that is not to be. Perhaps if I had hit you the other day and put you out of commission for a while, as I had hoped, as I did with Dove, then I could have spared you. But," she sighed philosophically, "that is not to be."

Lisa shivered at the finality in Mary's tone. She would kill them, as she had killed the others. "You can't get away with this," she said, her voice a soft whimper. "The police. They know, they . . ." Lisa's voice trailed off as she remembered how she had confided to Mary earlier that she had not called the police, had not called anyone, that no one knew she had come here tonight to get Dove's father's journal, except Dove, who was, by now, sleeping a deep Demerol-induced sleep.

"Lisa, dear, you would never have made a good detective. Although you'd like to think you would. You trusted people too much."

The past tense touched Lisa like a cold hand on her heart. "It's true, I trusted you. I believed you were the kind of person you pretended to be, a person of integrity and high moral principles," Lisa parried, partly because it was true and partly because, as she was beginning to realize, the only hope they had, and a slim one it was, was to keep Mary from killing them for as long as possible.

Mary rose to the bait. "It is my sense of morality that has forced me to kill," she insisted in a voice that demanded approval. "Sheldon Silverman and Louis Hammer deserved to die."

Lisa began to speak, but Mary interrupted her and said with a dismissive wave of her hand, "All right, I know what you're going to say—that you two don't deserve to die. Well, I'm truly sorry I must do this, but I can't have you telling the authorities what you know. And I will have to silence Dove as well, which I'm particularly sorry about, but she will have made the connection, too. And that will never do." Mary continued to slap the journal thoughtfully against her hand. She seemed to be undecided still.

"I don't know what connection you're talking about," Lisa said. "Dove didn't have any suspicions about you. I know that. She would have told me so. Dove really likes you and trusts you."

Mary said, "I'm sorry, but I can't take chances. Dove is the most dangerous remaining witness of all. She's read the journal. If she hasn't made the connection yet, I'm sure she will."

"How did you know about Jim Kent's journal?" Lisa asked. "Dove told me that she had never told anyone about it except Sam."

"She didn't tell me about the journal," Mary said, "but she told me she had found something, something that had been lost and that changed her whole life. I knew she meant her father's journal."

How did Mary know there was a journal? Lisa wondered, but she didn't pursue it. Instead, she decided to appeal to Mary's sense of morality again. She tried to speak jauntily, as she had when they were friends. "Look, Mary, so far you've killed only two bad guys. If you stopped now, you will have done what was morally necessary. And you will not have harmed any innocent people. Sam and I will not tell about this. Right, Sam?"

"Absolutely."

Mary gave her a sharp look. "I've been accused of many things in my day, but never of stupidity," she said.

"You know you won't be able to live with yourself if you do this," Lisa said.

"Let us go and we'll testify on your behalf," Sam put in.

"I'm doing only what I have to do. It's your lives or mine. I promise your deaths will be painless," Mary said.

Lisa sighed. Mary certainly was not stupid. She and Sam were doomed unless help came or, somehow, they managed to escape.

Back to stalling, Lisa thought, trying to keep panic away. By now she was too frightened to be curious, but she asked, "Why? Why did you kill them? And what is this connection

you keep talking about, that nobody seems to have made but
you?"

Mary was assiduously wiping off fingerprints all over the
room. She didn't answer.

Lisa persisted, "What's in that deadly little book other
than Kent's referring to his guilt about Sam's messed-up experiment? What does any of it have to do with you, anyway?"

Now Mary was fiddling with the knobs on the old gas
stove in a way that made Lisa begin to tremble. She couldn't
seem to stop her jaw from shaking, causing her teeth to chat-
ter. Her mind kept scampering ahead, like a rabbit in a hole,
trying to find a way out.

"Aren't you at least going to explain what this is all
about?" Sam asked.

Mary checked her watch. "I don't have much time," she
said, "but I am going to explain." She took the little notebook
from her capacious pocketbook, opened it, flipped some
pages. She seemed to know what she was looking for. Finding
it, she began to read in the beautiful lilting voice that Lisa had
so admired: " 'Danny Connors is a true revolutionary. Makes
Shel look like the phony he is. Danny grew up in Londonderry, Derry he calls it, Northern Ireland, in the midst of the
Troubles. Over there, being a Catholic means you're a born
fighter. He's our bomb expert. Grew up making Molotov cocktails in milk bottles.' " Here a gentle smile played over Mary's
features. " 'Yet, he's as gentle and loving as a baby. He's got a
young sister back home named, you guessed it, Brigid. She's
brilliant, he tells me. He showed me her picture. Even though
she's still only a kid, she's a knockout. Gorgeous red hair and
the same almond-shaped butterscotch-colored eyes he's got.
But Brigid's got a scar on her right temple shaped like a star

that she got in the bombing of a pub in which their parents were killed. She's all he's got now and he adores her. He sends her most of his fellowship money so she can stay in school. She wants to go on to college, wants to be a professor of literature. He's hoping she'll be able to come to the U.S. for college, wherever he's doing his work. Maybe here at Page if he stays. Believe me, I'd be happy if my Little Dove turned out like Danny's Brigid . . .' " Mary stopped reading and looked up at them. Her eyes were filled with tears.

"He sounds like a wonderful person, Danny. Your brother?" Sam asked.

Mary nodded.

Lisa remembered how Mary had dispelled her suspicions by telling her that she had grown up in Dublin and had never even heard of Danny Connors, who came from Derry. She wondered how Mary had changed from Brigid Connors to Mary Reardon. "Your brother would never have approved of the murder of innocent people," she tried.

"Be quiet," Mary said firmly. "Do you want me to continue or not?" She glared at Lisa in a way she never had before.

"Please go on," Sam said.

Mary turned some more pages until she found what she wanted. She read: " 'April 30, 1968. Dear God, help us to perform our mission well. Tonight Danny cried on my shoulder. He's scared. I reassured him, but I'm just as scared. I've thought deeply about our plan and I know I must go ahead with it. We must make a start. If we don't speak out, who will? All Danny talked about was Brigid. If anything happens to him, she'll not be able to afford college unless she can get a scholarship, and they're damned hard to come by. He made me promise I'd help her if he doesn't make it. We're both worried about Shel, worried about whether he has the dedication necessary for this operation, despite his big talk.' "

Mary looked over at them, eyes huge and bright with tears.

"Danny wasn't killed in the explosion," Lisa remembered out loud. "But he was tried and found guilty of murder, sentenced to twenty-five years in Attica. He was killed there in the prison revolt in September 1971."

Mary was sobbing gently now.

"But surely you wouldn't harm Jim Kent's daughter," Lisa pleaded. "Jim Kent was Danny's friend. He loved Danny like a brother. He promised to help you. If he hadn't been killed . . ."

Mary had herself in control now. "I told you before. I feel particularly sorry about Dove," she said in a hard, brisk voice. "I thought that putting her in the hospital and getting my hands on this journal would take care of everything. But then you two had to show up and ruin my plan. Anyway, I was worried that Dove already knew too much. You see, I knew a great deal about what was in Kent's journal because he used to read it to Danny and then Danny would write me about it. As soon as I realized Dove had found the journal, I knew I had to do something about her. If she hasn't figured out yet that I'm Danny Connors's sister, she will soon enough. The description of my scar alone would alert anyone."

Lisa looked at Mary's scar. It didn't look like a star to her, more like a lopsided spider. She had once asked Mary about it, and Mary had explained she'd gotten it in a fall from a bicycle when she was a kid. Lisa would never have made the connection; she doubted that Dove would. "Mary, no one would . . ."

"Be quiet. I'm thinking." Mary continued to plan, thinking aloud. "Even though I kill you two, making it look as if

Sam killed Lisa and then himself, I may still be at risk. If I re-move all the incriminating pages and leave the journal here, then the police will figure out that Sam must have killed Sil-verman and Hammer, then killed Lisa and finally himself."

She looked thoughtfully at Lisa. "The police will believe that you found the journal and read it." She waved her hand in the way Lisa had seen her do so often when she was think-ing out a problem. "That Sam discovered you here reading the journal and thought he had to kill you to keep his secret safe."

Sam interrupted, "Then why would I kill myself?"

Mary laughed. "Why indeed," she said. She seemed re-lieved to be working it all out. "Fear of apprehension. Self-disgust. After all, you've killed a lot of people," Mary chided pleasantly.

"Too many," Lisa said. "They'll find out. You can't have covered yourself completely."

Sam, inspired, added, "You were so concerned about Dove's realizing that you were Danny Connors's sister just by reading those pages that referred to you. What about the po-lice? They're not fools."

Mary laughed again. "Ah, but I'm going to destroy the pages that refer to Danny having a sister."

"But, don't you see, the police will trace everyone involved in that bombing in 1968," Sam said. "Their families, anyone who might have reason to hate Silverman and Hammer. They'll find out that you're Danny Connors's sister, they'll find out your real name. They're very good at that kind of thing."

Are they? Lisa wondered. Lieutenant Cohen had been so quick to accept the suicide note, the arranged clues. She looked away so that Mary couldn't read the doubt in her eyes.

CHAPTER 26

At that moment at Braeton Police Headquarters Lieutenant
Cohen was taking the suicide note from his locked file. He
read it yet another time.

"Murderer of three," he repeated to himself. "In my judgement Silverman deserved to die. He was the murderer of
three."

Unlikely that Hammer would have used those words.
When Hammer called Silverman a murderer, he would have
been thinking only of the two men who died in the explosion
in the Lohr Science Center on that May night in 1968, the
two whose deaths Silverman had been responsible for. The
third man did not die that night. The third man, Daniel
Connors, was sentenced to twenty-five years in Attica. And
he died there three years later, one of the inmates caught in
the crossfire between the prisoners and the New York State
Police.

Cohen felt certain now that the writer of the suicide note
had not been Louis Hammer. Hammer might or might not
have seen the name of Daniel Connors listed in the newspaper
as one of the prisoners killed in the riot. But even if he had, it

was unlikely that he would have considered Silverman responsible for Connors's death. No, thought Cohen, "murderer of three" would be the term used by someone who was aware of the fate of Daniel Connors, someone who cared very much about what happened to him, who would have followed carefully the events that led to Connors's death and, therefore, put the blame on Silverman.

Everything about the letter seemed wrong to Cohen now. It explained too much, and yet not enough. It seemed self-conscious, as if trying to make a point, not like the agonized cry of someone about to kill himself.

And, Cohen thought, it seemed unlikely that a man whose conscience would allow him to be quiet at the trial of Daniel Connors, to blackmail Silverman for years, and finally to try to steal Silverman's girlfriend as recently as last summer would suddenly have a crisis of conscience, would write, "I can no longer endure the empty lie my life has become," and then shoot himself in the head with the same gun with which he had shot his victim, right on the eve of the tenure vote that meant so much to him.

There could be only one person who would refer to Silverman as the murderer of three. It seemed so obvious to him now that he couldn't imagine why he hadn't figured it out sooner.

The telephone rang. He grabbed it in the middle of the ring and barked, "Cohen."

The line was heavy with static. "Donaghue here." A weary voice. "I've been trying for hours, but the transatlantic lines from the little country towns are chancy at best. So I had to drive back to Dublin, and even from here it's been a long wait to get through. But thank God I've gotten through to ye at last."

Cohen was aware that from where Donaghue was calling it was early morning and that the man was exhausted. Still he couldn't control his impatience. "Brian, what have you got for me?" There would be time for thank-you's later.

He and Brian Donaghue, his counterpart on the Dublin police force, had done many such favors for each other over the years. Even though they'd never met, there had been several cases on which they had worked together most satisfactorily. It was Brian who had found the certificate of death for Brigid Connors in the Dublin records department when Cohen was checking on the survivors of those harmed by the Page bombing.

"I don't know that I found much," Brian was saying. "I hope it helps ye." His sigh sounded, through the static, like deep ocean water lapping at the cable.

"Go on," Cohen said eagerly.

Brian began, "I started out in Dublin. I located Doctor Michael Gerry, who signed Brigid Connors's death certificate. He remembered when I showed him a copy of the certificate, although he could not describe the girl. Very sad, he said. She was only nineteen when she died of tuberculosis."

"Can these death certificates be forged or tampered with in any way?" Cohen asked.

"Not bloody likely. I checked on Gerry. Perfectly respectable. And, as I say, he remembered the case."

"Go on," Cohen said impatiently.

Brian went on, "Then I went over to Trinity College. Their records on Mary Reardon fit perfectly with the information you gave me. She entered the college in September of 1972 on scholarship. She had an outstanding record, went on until she received a D. Phil. in Irish Literature. Then she became an instructor and later a professor. Very unusual to be

hired on like that, especially for a woman. I talked to someone in the Literature Department I know who said she was
very capable, well thought of. I could find nothing amiss."

"I see." Cohen was trying to absorb this information, to fit
it to the contours of his suspicions.

Brian continued, "Then I flew up to Derry, rented a car,
and drove to the village on the Foyle River where Brigid and
Daniel Connors were born. Loughinnis. I found records there
of the births. Daniel Connors, October 10, 1944 and Brigid
Eileen Connors, April 1, 1952 to Daniel and Eileen Connors.
At first I could find no one in Loughinnis who remembered
any of the Connorses. I went to the address given on the birth
certificates, a poor farm in the hills. The family living there
had never heard of the Connorses and they had lived there for
twenty years. Then I was told that a Father Feeley, who had
been the village priest for many years and had retired to a little
house nearby, would be the person to ask. So I visited him. He
did remember the Connorses. Said they had never been able to
make a go of it on the farm and had moved to Derry in the
mid-fifties with the two children. Then he heard through others that the parents had been killed in a pub bombing, not an
unusual event in Derry, unfortunately. Father Feeley knew
nothing about what had become of the children."

"Did you get a description of Brigid Connors?" Cohen interrupted.

"Yes. I did that. Even though the old priest is nearly blind
now, he said he had a sharp picture of little Brigid in his
mind with her fiery red hair and golden eyes. He never saw
her after the family moved to Derry when she was a wee girl."

Cohen asked, "And Mary Reardon? You went to her home
town?"

"I did. I flew back to Dublin and drove out to Mayhill,

about thirty miles outside town. There I had no trouble finding Mary Reardon's birth certificate in the town hall. Born Mary May Reardon, January 21, 1950. I found records of the deaths of her parents and two infant sisters. I found birth certificates for two older brothers. I asked around town and found out that the brothers had moved away long ago, after their parents died."

Cohen could hardly contain himself now. "But the description—the description of Mary Reardon—you got it?"

"Oh, sure and I did, several times over. I found a neighbor and Mary Reardon's old elementary school teacher and . . ."

"What did she look like?"

"One of those pretty little Irish girls. Small and thin with the black hair and green eyes that have made our girls famous all over . . ."

"You're sure about that description?"

"Sure and I'm sure. There were a few left who remembered little Mary Reardon and the tragedy of her parents' death in an automobile accident. They thought she had moved on to Australia with one of the older brothers, but no one was sure where she went."

Cohen sighed, a deep sigh in which weariness and relief were mixed. "Thanks so much for all you've done," he said. "You've given me just what I needed. I do appreciate your going so much out of your way to get it."

"Think nothing of it. You'd do the same for me. You have done. We come out even."

Cohen laughed. "I think you've cracked our case. I'll write you the details. Just send a bill as usual for your expenses."

CHAPTER 27

Mary was leaning on the kitchen table, a wild, gleeful look in her eyes. "I'll tell you two something that I swore I would never reveal to a living soul. But I can tell you. Now."

The ominousness of her words struck Lisa like a blow. Mary no longer considered Sam and her as living souls.

Mary said, almost in a whisper, "Brigid Connors is dead. I went to her funeral."

At their puzzled looks, she smiled. "When Danny was sentenced to prison," she began, "I lost everything. I had to drop out of school. I couldn't find work in Derry. I went to Dublin, worked as a barmaid in a pub, cleaned bathrooms, whatever I could get. Sometimes I begged. I sent every penny I could to pay for Danny's appeal. I asked everyone I met to help. No one would. No one cared. I had no family. What few friends I had disappeared when I needed them. I sold my clothes, any little trinkets I had. Until I had nothing left to sell. Nothing but myself. Can you understand how dehumanizing that is? Believe me, death is better.

"It was then that I met Mary Reardon. She was only two years older than I, but she was desperately ill with TB. Sick though she was, she also sold the only asset she had—her body. She let me share her dank little basement room. She was the only human being who showed me any kindness.

"Less than two weeks after I learned that Danny had been killed in the prison revolt, Mary died. She was so emaciated that she was unrecognizable and, besides, there was no one to recognize her. Like me, she had no family. No friends. She had been born outside of Dublin. Her parents had been killed in an auto crash. Her brothers had moved to Australia. So I took her identification and I buried her in my name. All I had to worry about was remembering that I was now two years older. The death certificate of Brigid Eileen Connors is on file in Dublin." She gave a bitter laugh. "Since Danny was dead, I didn't have to earn money for his appeal, so I applied for a scholarship at Trinity College. When, finally, I was awarded my scholarship and continued my education, it was in her name. So you see, if the police do trace Brigid Connors, they will find out that she died of tuberculosis in Dublin in 1971."

"When you assumed Mary Reardon's identity, were you planning, even then, to kill Silverman?" Lisa asked.

"Silverman and Hammer," Mary answered without hesitation. "Of course, it was Silverman I wanted the most, and I wanted him to pay for what he had done to Danny. I wanted to punish him, and I did."

Lisa shuddered, remembering the sight of Silverman's mutilated body.

"As for Hammer, since he, also, deserved to die, I planned that he would—how do you say it, Lisa?—take the rap for me."

"Why did he deserve to die?" Sam asked.

"Hammer's lie might have cost Danny his life. If the judge

and jury had believed Danny that Silverman was posted outside the science center to prevent anyone from coming in and,
possibly, getting hurt, maybe they would've given Danny a
lighter sentence, maybe he would've been home safely before
that prison uprising. But neither Silverman nor Hammer
cared what happened to Danny. And so, he died, the only person who ever meant anything to me."

"Dove's life was ruined, too," Lisa said quickly. "Her father died in that explosion and, later, her mother committed
suicide."

"I'm sorry about that," Mary said simply.

"How can you kill all of us just to protect yourself?" Lisa
asked. "It's one thing killing those two rats who caused
Danny's death. But we're innocent. We would have loved
Danny if we knew him. Listening to Jim Kent's voice
through the journal, I know he loved Danny like a brother."

Mary shook her head and said coldly, "I've made my decision. I'm going to live. I will kill anyone who stands in
the way of my freedom. I've given up enough. I had to
avenge Danny's murder—for that's what it was, murder—
and I feel better for it, freer. I'm sorry I have to sacrifice
you, Lisa, because I've really enjoyed knowing you. And
you're right, it will trouble me to have killed you two,
and especially Dove, but it would trouble me more to give
up my life or my liberty."

"Please, Mary, we'll help you escape," Lisa begged.

Mary smiled bitterly. "You, of all people, must know I am
not that naive."

"What will you do with us?" Sam asked.

"I assure you your deaths will not be painful," Mary said.
"First, I must finish going through the journal and remove
those pages that allude to me. What remains will, I think,

provide the police with a sufficient motive for you to have killed Lisa and taken your own life. They will see that your anger at Silverman for ruining your career grew to unmanageable proportions when Silverman was appointed to the Finstermann Chair. And your misery at the failure of your work became too great to control."

"Failure? Thanks a lot," Sam said. "I am—was—still hoping for tenure on the basis of that work."

Mary laughed. "Should I say possible failure? Is that better?"

"Slightly. By what means will you kill us?" Sam asked.

"I shall simply turn on the gas stove without lighting it and you will die peacefully, painlessly. Like Sylvia Plath," Mary said encouragingly, turning to Lisa.

"I don't want to die," Lisa pleaded.

"But surely when the police come, they'll see that I couldn't have committed murder and then suicide tied to a chair like this," Sam said sensibly.

"Of course not. I'll turn the gas on before I leave. After I've taken care of Dove, I'll come back and untie you, Sam. Now I must change into my nurse's uniform. I have to arrive at the hospital at exactly eleven o'clock so that I'll be unnoticed in the shift changeover."

"But what about Dove's death? They'll know that was murder," Lisa said.

"A severely injured patient slipping into unconsciousness and suffocating in her bedclothes? I think it will be considered accidental," Mary said as she left the kitchen.

The clock on the kitchen wall showed 10:05. Lisa struggled against her bonds, but Mary had been very efficient. Sam was tied to his chair with clothesline on top of the socks. Now Lisa knew why Mary had been so careful to tie the ropes over the socks on Sam's wrists and ankles. She didn't want any marks to show that he had been tied up when he died.

"What are we going to do?" Lisa whispered.

"We'll do something," Sam promised. Just the slow, even tempo of his words reassured her.

"Sam."

He looked at her with steady brown eyes.

"Sam, why didn't you tell me you talked with Dove yesterday? Why didn't you tell me about Jim Kent's journal, that you were looking for it?"

"It seems really stupid now, Lisa, but when Dove called me yesterday at lunchtime and said she wanted to come over and talk to me about Jim Kent, it was like all those horrible years at Page were about to be replayed. Like I was on that roller coaster ride straight down."

"What do you mean?"

"Well, when the phone rang, I was looking over the summary I've been working on of my study to present with the rest of my credentials to the tenure committee. I was rewriting the section on projected results and cursing my bad luck that the results were not developing as I'd hoped. When Dove told me that she was the daughter of Jim Kent who had died in the blast at the Lohr Science Center in 1968, the same explosion that had destroyed my nearly completed experiment, I told her I couldn't see her.

"Then she told me that she had the journal her father had kept during the time he was planning the bombing, that I was mentioned in it, that her father had written of how the blast would surely ruin my experiment, how angry I would be."

"And you were."

"Sure I was angry. At the time it was as if my whole world

had blown up along with my experiment. Jane and Eric gone. And then my work. Everything—even all my records gone, as if they had never existed. It was too much."

"I understand that. What I don't see is why it affected you so much now, sixteen years later."

Sam laughed bitterly. "It's just what Mary figured—I knew I'd be a suspect. Silverman had been murdered on the very day his appointment to the Finstermann Chair was announced, then Hammer. It wasn't certain if the crime was murder-suicide or if some third person had murdered the two of them. And here was this girl—a ghost from the past as far as I was concerned—with evidence, written evidence that I was harmed, seriously harmed, by that explosion which destroyed my experiment."

Lisa was beginning to understand.

"And I thought that if that became known around here, people might think—the Braeton police might think—just as Mary realized as soon as she saw it, that I might have murdered Silverman and Hammer, that my original fury was rekindled when Silverman was appointed to the Finstermann Chair. Can you imagine what effect my being a murder suspect would have on that tenure committee?"

"I can imagine," Lisa said.

"It would be just the excuse they'd need to turn me down. And I thought it was only a question of time before the journal got to the authorities."

He's right, Lisa thought. It would be just what they needed. And it had been a break for him that Dove was hurt and hospitalized. It prevented her from telling others at Addison that her father had written in his journal that Sam would be angry if his experiment was destroyed. So, as it turned out, Sam even had a motive for injuring Dove. And as soon as he found out that Dove was in the hospital, he'd come over to look for the journal.

As if he knew what she was thinking, he said, "I was very sorry when I heard Dove was hurt, but it seemed like the perfect opportunity to take a look at the journal, see how damaging it was."

"I suppose you would have destroyed it if you found it."

Sam looked pained. "You mean the journal?"

"Or the part that mentioned you."

"I honestly don't know what I would've done, Lisa. I knew how important that little book was to the girl. I think I just wanted to see it, to see for myself how damaging it was to me. I had some idea of going to her when she felt better and telling her how important it was to me that no one saw that part, at least until after next week. Did you really think I would destroy it?"

"I'm sorry, Sam," Lisa said. A feeling of emptiness momentarily replaced her fear.

"I should have told you," Sam said, "about my talk with Dove. And I should have told you what I was looking for."

"Yes." Lisa sighed. Despair made her weak. "You didn't trust me. I didn't trust you. Some basis for a relationship."

Sam said slowly, "I wanted to tell you. I was afraid I'd lose you." He laughed ironically. "There I was, too old for you, too fat for you. I didn't want you to think that maybe I was also a murderer."

Lisa didn't laugh. She had thought so. "Oh, Sam," she said. She couldn't say any more.

Now, in what she thought of as the last moments of her life, everything was suddenly painfully clear. She didn't love Sam. She never had. She liked him. She liked being with him. She felt sorry for him. But, most of all, she liked his caring for her. She had been attracted to Brad, who wasn't good for her. Sam, who was good for her, didn't attract her enough. She sighed deeply. There was so much about human feelings, especially her own, she couldn't understand. And now it was too late. She felt tears building up behind her eyes. Her nose ached. She didn't want to cry.

"It's all right, Lisa dear, we'll get away somehow," Sam said soothingly. But she could hear the lack of conviction in his voice. He was trying to give her comfort right up to the end. A truly considerate man. Better than she ever deserved, yet he wasn't what she wanted. "Thanks, Sam," she said in a husky whisper. "Thanks for everything." She wouldn't give in to tears. She'd follow his example.

CHAPTER 28

Mary entered the kitchen briskly. She was wearing a nurse's uniform of the baggy figure-concealing variety. Her striking auburn hair was hidden by a gray wig, tied back in a bun and crowned by a starched cap. She work pink-tinted glasses with steel frames, white stockings, and white rubber-soled shoes. You wouldn't look at her twice if you saw her walking purposefully down a hospital corridor.

"Well, saying your good-byes?" she asked in a voice that fit the part, crisp and clear.

"Look at you, a regular Florence Nightingale," Sam said in disgust.

Lisa thought of Mary's efficiency. So many times before she had admired her for it. Now the knowledge of how capable the woman was filled her with dread. "You won't get away with it. Dove has a nurse with her."

"She has a nurse who's in and out of her room. I've been there, too, don't forget. Now don't try to delay me," Mary said, moving rapidly across the room. "I feel very badly about this. I've already told you so."

"Not as badly as we do," Sam said.

"I should have gagged you; then I wouldn't have to listen to this," Mary said, leaning over the stove. "But I was afraid that if you died breathing through your noses, the police surgeon could tell in the postmortem that you'd been gagged."

Neither Sam nor Lisa answered.

She's as cold-blooded as a python, Lisa was thinking. That warmth of hers was only an act. No, she corrected herself, she really did like me. She doesn't want to kill me. But she's obsessed with avenging her brother's death. With saving herself. So she can make up for all she's missed. And anything that gets in her way will be destroyed—just the way I put D-Con in back of my closets to get rid of mice. Lisa shivered. Mary was crazy. Dove had had as terrible a life as Mary had, yet she wasn't crazy. But Mary was insane. This cold-bloodedness without remorse must be insanity.

"I've been trying to figure out how you did it, how you . . ." Sam began.

But Mary cut in ruthlessly, "Be quiet. I've no time for this."

"So, a dying man has the right to no final requests? That is your idea of justice?" Sam spoke calmly.

Mary sighed, turned from the stove, consulted her watch. "All right," she said, the stern nurse allowing her patient one little whim only. "Five minutes. I know you're stalling for time. But I want to have as little on my conscience as possible."

Lisa started to say something but stopped when she caught Sam's eye.

Sam began eagerly, with a look of intense curiosity. "The suicide note. How did you manage that—the typing, the signature, the fingerprints and all, so that the police experts accepted it as the real thing?"

Mary said proudly, "It took a great deal of planning, believe me. Lou Hammer made it possible when he had himself appointed chairman of the faculty lecture committee because he was trying to make himself necessary to the department in the hope that he would obtain tenure. I got myself on his committee." She laughed. "That part was easy. I was the only faculty member. No one else in the English Department would serve on his committee because he was such an incompetent. Once on the committee, it was easy to arrange papers for his signature so that he signed a blank sheet, one that I had been able to take from his typewriter so that I knew it had his fingerprints on it.

"Wasn't it hard to arrange the sheets so that he thought he was signing a letter?"

Mary looked gleeful. "I got him in the habit of signing duplicate letters as I held them on my clipboard, fanlike. I pretended it was to save his valuable time. Gave him a feeling of importance. And if he had looked through them and seen a blank sheet, I could've pretended it was a mistake. The only hard part was keeping my prints off the damn paper. I solved that problem by managing to catch him out in the parking lot one day last month when it was still cold and I had my gloves on.

"The rest of it was easy. He had a Smith-Corona portable that he often brought in to the office. I slipped a duplicate key to his office off the board in the custodian's office. Then I waited for an evening when the typewriter was in his office and no one was in the English Department. I'd rehearsed the letter so often that it was a simple matter to type it out quickly with my gloves on. After that, of course, he would type on the machine again, and his prints would be the only ones on it.

"I called him up at three A.M. on the morning after Silverman's body was discovered and I put on a great act of fear and uncertainty, telling him I'd been up all night worrying about some evidence I had about Silverman's murder and I didn't know whether to go to the police with it and could he help me. Naturally, I knew he considered himself a prime suspect and he never dreamed I could be dangerous. So he told me to come right over with it and we'd talk. I asked him to let me in the back way. The rest is history."

"Very clever," Sam said with apparent appreciation. "But what about the gun? Where did you get it?"

Mary smiled at him. "You also are very clever, playing on my vanity to keep me talking, but your time is up." She walked back to the stove and started fiddling again. "The gun was my grandfather's. It was issued to him by the English when he fought with them in World War Two, the kind of gun many American soldiers brought home as souvenirs. I smuggled it into the country in my carry-on luggage. That was a bit tricky. Took some Irish charm," she said, her back to them.

She turned away from the stove and walked quickly to the kitchen door on her silent rubber heels. For a moment the only noise in the room was the slow, lazy hissing sound of gas escaping from the jet, a sound like that of a poisonous snake, coiled, taking its time, yet ready to spring.

"No. Don't do it," Lisa shouted, hysteria edging her words. "You won't be able to live with youself. We won't tell. Please."

The only answer to her shouts was the soft click of the kitchen door latch as the door shut tightly, leaving Lisa and Sam alone in the sealed room. As soon as the door closed, Lisa began to smell the faint sickly-sweet odor of gas.

The noise of Mary's car engine starting drowned out the sinister hissing for a few moments. The engine roared, tires crunched on pine cones in the driveway. For a few moments longer they heard the sounds of the car as it drove along the dirt road; then they could hear nothing but the steady release of gas into the enclosed room.

"I'm going to try to break the chair leg," Sam said. "If I could just move from this spot, I could break the window and at least get us some fresh air to counteract the effect of the gas."

With all his might he braced his leg against the chair leg. His face grew red with the effort, cords stood out in his neck. He pressed as hard as he could, bending his knee, pushing back against the slats that braced the wooden chair legs.

Lisa heard a splintering. One of the slats had broken. But the chair leg was firmly in place. Sam tried harder. His face turned from red to purple. Finally he gasped, "No leverage. Damn."

Lisa stopped fighting against the tightly knotted socks that bound her wrists. She tried to breathe as little as possible. The air was becoming heavy. Behind her eyes a dull ache throbbed.

Sam was still struggling. At least his groans covered the sound of the gas as it filled the room relentlessly with death.

Suddenly there was a crash and a cry of pain as Sam's chair fell to the floor.

"Sam. Sam, are you all right?"

Bitterly, he laughed. "If you call this all right. I hit my head. But I'll live. Hah!"

"Oh, Sam." Sadly Lisa looked over at the dear man who was still trying to make her laugh. In fact, he looked ridiculous, laughable, if one were in the mood to laugh. He had kicked the chair out of balance. It had fallen straight backward onto the floor. He lay on his back, tied in the chair, his legs still firmly fastened to the chair legs, which were intact. Only one slat was splintered.

"Those Yankees sure knew how to make furniture," Sam said. He was still struggling, but Lisa had the feeling that his efforts were only for show, to give her hope.

She said nothing more. What was there to say? She wanted to tell Sam to stop the struggle, to just relax. She worried about how uncomfortable he was in that awful position and still fighting. But maybe it was better this way—to go out fighting. "Do not go gentle into that good night. Rage, rage against the dying of the light." Death would take him in the midst of his fighting. He wouldn't even feel its cold hand.

Her headache seemed to be coming from somewhere deep inside her head, pulsing and undulating like a subterranean river. Was it true that death by gas was painless, as they said? Perhaps she would be drawn into that pulsing dark river and float there until she was pulled in among soft weeds and darting fish, then down, down into the dark stillness.

"Lisa!" Sam was calling to her urgently.

"What?"

"Try, Lisa. Try. Kick at your chair leg as I'm doing. It's flimsier than mine. You can break it. I know you can. Then you could hobble over here and work on my knots."

Lisa made some halfhearted attempts while Sam watched and encouraged. "It's no use," she said after a while. "I can't get any leverage." A pause, then, "Sam. Thanks."

"Lisa. I love you."

"Sam. I love you. But I'm not in love with you. Even in death I must be honest."

"It's okay."

CHAPTER 29

At Braeton police headquarters the phone rang again. Cohen snatched up the receiver. It was Hughes. "Lieutenant, you better get over here to the Rideways' right away. Jencks brought his analysis kit. And it checks out. It's the car, all right. Registered to Thomas Rideway, son of Professor and Mrs. Elliot Rideway. The family is in Europe this year on sabbatical. Car's stored here in the carriage house."

"Is she back yet?"

"Not yet."

"I'll be right there."

As he drove toward the Rideways' house in the hilly section of West Braeton, Cohen envisioned the strong features of the handsome red-haired Irishwoman and shook his head sadly.

CHAPTER 30

Sam had managed to turn on his side and didn't seem quite as uncomfortable. They looked at each other. Silently. Then Sam smiled.

As Lisa tried to smile back, she saw an image in her mind of the phony suicide letter. And in a flash, she knew what was wrong with it. "Judgement," she said aloud, seeing the word as she had seen it on the sheet of paper Lieutenant Cohen had held out to her. "Judgement" is the British spelling. In America the word is spelled "judgment." No *e* after the *g*.

She said to Sam, "The suicide note. She spelled judgment with an *e*. That's the British way. How could I have been so stupid? I should have known."

Now she felt a burst of energy, like a runner who has run to the point of exhaustion and then, without warning, experiences a sudden spurt of strength, a confidence in his capacity. She wrenched and pulled at her bonds. Something wet trickled down her hands. She knew it must be blood, but she had lost all feeling in her hands. "Judgment," she said again. The knots were firmly tied. Her hands were slippery with blood, but she fought on.

"A piece of yarn has come loose," she called to Sam. He wasn't moving. His eyes were barely open. He seemed to be breathing with difficulty.

"Sam. Sam. Wake up, don't give up."

Sam opened his eyes. "I haven't given up." His voice was blurred. His big chest moved slowly. Up. Down. Up. Down.

Lisa pulled at the yarn frantically, her fingers so slippery that she kept losing her grip. Her nails were ragged and torn.

"Talk to me," she shouted, as she saw Sam's eyes closing again. She knew nothing about how a person died of gas poisoning, but she remembered a cautionary tale about how you should never fall asleep in the snow, and she thought, somehow, it might apply. "Talk to me."

"What more can I say," Sam said. She didn't know whether or not he was trying to be funny. His breathing was harsh and labored. Lisa laughed without mirth. She herself felt drugged, her eyelids longing to give in to the heavy pull of gravity. Then abruptly she stopped laughing. "Oh, I've come to the knot. I don't know if I can unravel any more." Her fingers scrabbled on the unyielding surface of the tightly knotted yarn. Despair filled her. Tears started in her eyes. "Oh, Sam," she wailed.

Sam's eyes slowly opened. She watched them try to focus on her, try to take in what was happening. "You can do it," he said in a slow, husky voice. "You can. You must."

She began to work even harder at the knots. Slowly she could feel the material giving way. Thank God, Mary underestimated me and didn't tie clothesline over the socks on my wrists the way she did on Sam's, she thought, or it would all be over. The little bit of hope seemed to give her strength. She worked out the first knot, then unraveled yarn to the second knot. She couldn't believe it as she felt the knot pull loose and her wrists come free. I did it. I did it. She didn't know whether she spoke the words aloud. Sam seemed inert. She tried to rub the circulation back into her hands. It seemed to take a long time to free her ankles with her numbed fingers. Too long. Panic seized her. Oh, please, please, she whispered. Sam lay still. "Sam. I'm coming," she called as she loosened the ties at last.

She sprang from her chair to the stove, head whirling. She turned off the gas jet, threw open the window with such force that the window rope snapped. Sam's chair was near the back door. She opened the door and, with all her strength, dragged him outside, over the raised threshold into the back-yard.

Sam was not unconscious. As the first rush of cool night air touched him, his eyes slid open. He started to take huge, shivering gulps of air.

She untied him and helped him sit up. They were both dizzy and weak. "Are you all right?" she asked, aware of her thick, croaking voice. Each breath was painful. But she was alive. They were alive.

Sam nodded. They sat on the cold, wet grass. Lisa looked up at a spectacular sky—black velvet with millions of twinkling stars. "My head," she moaned. A sudden flow of memory brought tears to her eyes. "Dove. Oh God, Dove. We have to hurry. Mary's going to kill her."

Sam groaned, his chest heaving. "Call," he moaned. Clearly, he couldn't move.

Again, Lisa felt a spurt of energy. She staggered back to the house. Raced through the kitchen. There was only a slight odor of gas in the living room because Mary had closed the kitchen door when she had left them there to die. Lisa dialed "O". "This is an emergency," she said. "I must reach Braeton General Hospital."

She heard the ringing and then the same switchboard operator answered in her singsong voice.

"This is an emergency," Lisa repeated. "A patient is in grave danger. Dove Kent in room A-103. Quickly, connect me with the nurse's station there."

Immediately she heard a buzzing. Sam lurched into the doorway. He stood uncertainly, a hand to his head.

"Hello." Jean's voice.

"It's Lisa Davis. Dove Kent is in serious danger. Someone dressed as a nurse is going to try to smother her."

"What?" Jean's voice went up three octaves.

"Please," Lisa begged. "Don't let anyone near her. Get help right away. I'm calling the police now."

"Okay," came the doubtful reply.

Lisa dialed the Braeton police. Lieutenant Cohen was not there. Neither was Officer Hughes. She gave the deskman her message. "It's urgent. Get to the hospital right away or Dove Kent will be murdered."

Lisa rushed to the front door. Sam followed slowly. "We'll take your car. It's closer," Lisa said, running toward the back of the house, pulling Sam along with her. She helped him into the passenger seat after opening the windows.

She sped down the driveway crunching gravel and pine cones. Then she barreled down the dirt road. On the main road into Braeton, she sat hunched forward in the driver's seat as the headlights pulled some order out of the dark night and the fresh air blowing in revived her. Her breathing was easier, but the pounding headache remained. Only a part of her mind paid attention to the driving. She was remembering how she had liked Mary. Mary's smile. Her humor. Her quick soft hand patting Lisa's shoulder, even her cheek. Lisa shuddered.

Beside her Sam was beginning to come to life. "Oh, my head," he moaned. He sat up with a start and asked, "Lisa, you all right?" in his old protective tone. Then he began to remember. "Oh, my God," he said.

The five-minute drive to the hospital seemed like hours. Lisa didn't know what she would find when she got there. Would Jean follow her instructions? Would the desk sergeant at Braeton police headquarters send someone over immediately? It was dark and still in front of the hospital, lit only by arched lights above the parking lot. Lisa parked in front of the main door beside a no-parking sign. She leapt out of the car, Sam following, and raced into the building.

CHAPTER 31

Lisa ran by the reception desk across the slickly polished tiles, Sam lumbering behind her. The receptionist called out, but they continued running, through the swinging doors, into the hospital corridor. Lisa dodged bunches of people as she raced toward Dove's room. The corridors were thronged. Nurses and orderlies arrived for the late-night shift as those who were finishing their duty prepared to leave. People looked after her curiously as she ran, leaving Sam far behind. A man in a white coat called after her, "Hey, this is a hospital."

The door to Dove's room was closed tightly. Lisa pushed at it. Encountering resistance, she pushed harder. The door opened with difficulty partway, blocked by something soft and inert. Lisa stepped over it without looking, but she knew it was a body. Her eyes were riveted to the hospital bed, where Mary stood over Dove holding the girl down with one hand while pressing a pillow over her face with the other. Dove's breath came in ragged gasps as she fought with all her strength for her life.

Lisa lunged at Mary and grabbed the arm that was holding

the pillow. Mary whirled toward her. Through the white powder on her face, her bronze eyes gleamed like lanterns through a mist. Her gray wig was askew, revealing her flaming widow's peak.

Mary wrested her arm free of Lisa's grip and pushed her hard in the chest with the strength of desperation. As Lisa tottered off balance, Mary grabbed the metal water pitcher from the bedside table and, in a rapid movement, struck at Lisa's head with it. Perhaps if she wasn't still weak, Lisa would have been able to hold her own with Mary, grab the arm with the pitcher, fight back. As it was, Lisa had all she could do to duck. The pitcher swished by her head, just missing the place above her left ear where Mary had hit her earlier. Off balance again, Lisa grabbed at Mary. But Lisa's hold barely deflected Mary's aim as she swung the pitcher again and hit Lisa this time on the other side of the head.

Lisa staggered and nearly fell as the room tipped dangerously. She found herself on her knees on the floor. Steadying herself on the metal bars of Dove's hospital bed, she saw Mary lift the pitcher again. Dizzily, Lisa ducked, covered her head with her arms. Too weak to do anything else, she slumped toward the floor awaiting the blow.

But the blow didn't come. Instead, over the pounding in her head, she heard loud noises and shouting. Mary dropped the pitcher. It clanged on the tiled floor. Looking across the spinning room, Lisa saw that help had arrived. A policeman was helping a groaning Jean Sullivan to her feet as Lieutenant Cohen and another policeman rushed into the room, guns drawn.

Strong arms lifted Lisa to her feet. Mary's arms. And she heard Mary's voice, icy and level, right behind her, close enough so that she felt the tickle of Mary's breath on her ear.

"Stop right there," Mary ordered the approaching policemen. "I have a knife pressed to her back and I won't hesitate to use it."

Lisa felt a sharp pressure at her back. She breathed in quickly and tried to focus her eyes. She caught a glimpse of Sam's worried face in the doorway, jostled aside by more uniformed men.

Mary held her by the arm as she pressed the knife against her. There was a heavy silence in the room. No one moved.

"I am leaving here," Mary announced into the silence. "Out the door behind me and down the fire escape to my car. You are not to follow. Lisa is coming with me and if I am hindered in any way, I will kill her. Is that clear?"

Lieutenant Cohen nodded slowly. "Clear. But I'll make a deal with you. Go. But leave her here. We won't stop you."

Mary's laugh rang in Lisa's ears. "No deals. We're going now. If I'm not bothered, she'll be alive. Otherwise . . ."

Lieutenant Cohen nodded again. Lisa met his moist red eyes, but could read nothing there.

Pulling Lisa with her, Mary started to back up toward the door to the balcony, keeping the knife firmly against Lisa's back. "Do exactly as I say," she warned.

Together they crossed the narrow balcony. Mary started carefully down the stairs holding Lisa close to her. "Move with me," she commanded. Lisa did as she was told, descending the stairs in rhythm with Mary's steps. She felt dizzy and weak. She wondered what would happen if she fainted. Would Mary just leave her and make a run for it or would she kill her before she went? Lisa shuddered at the thought of the sharp knife slicing into her flesh and then into her heart or a lung.

Mary felt her tremble and said, "Almost there."

"I'm going to . . . I think I . . ." Lisa began weakly as they reached the bottom of the stairs. She felt as if her legs were buckling under her.

"Better not," Mary threatened and held her arm tighter as she began to hurry her toward her car.

The fire escape had let them out near the service entrance of the hospital onto a graveled path. Lisa tripped and stumbled as Mary half-pushed her along the path. Out of the corner of her eye Lisa could see the people massed at the front entrance. Murmurs and exclamations reached her ears in waves like communications from another world. Lisa felt as if she were being taken away from this world, from everything she loved.

When they reached Mary's VW, Mary threw open the driver's door and pushed Lisa in. "Get over," she ordered, prodding her with the knife point.

Lisa clambered in, half-fell across the gearshift, and slumped into the passenger seat, her head resting on the window. Her scalp felt painful and sore where Mary had struck her. She put her hand up to touch it. The wound was caked with dried blood.

"Keep your hands down," Mary said. Lisa could see her eyes glittering with fear.

Lisa let her arm fall onto the seat, moaned, and closed her eyes. She was beginning to feel stronger; if she pretended to be semiconscious, maybe Mary wouldn't watch her so closely. Somehow she must escape. Lisa calculated her chances. Mary had planned her stratagem carefully. She had parked her car as close as possible to the fire exit to facilitate her escape. She must have entered the building through the service entrance and made her way up the back stairs to Dove's room. If Lisa hadn't alerted Jean Sullivan to the danger, Mary would have slipped unnoticed into the room, held the pillow over the sleeping girl's face, and been on her way in a matter of minutes. But Jean must have rushed into Dove's room after Lisa's telephone call and been knocked down by Mary before she could go for help.

The VW started up with a roar and lurched forward. Through slitted eyes, Lisa saw dark bushes hurtling by. Mary was driving fast down the short road lined with parked cars. Lisa figured that she was going to make a U-turn at the end of the road, which widened for just that purpose, rather than try to turn around in the narrow part of the road where she was parked. Mary would have to slow down to make the turn, Lisa thought. That's when she would make her move. Mary was driving fast. Both hands on the steering wheel. The knife she held in her right hand gleamed in the moonlight.

I'll have to be quick, Lisa thought. Be out and clear before that hand with the knife can get to me. There was no time to think it all through carefully. At least Mary had her eyes on the road. Groaning softly, rolling her head from side to side, Lisa could see that the passenger door was unlocked.

Mary reached the widest part of the turnaround, tires screeching on the asphalt surface as she began to turn, braking as she did so, her eyes on the road.

Lisa felt for the door handle. Now I must do it. Now. Or the chance will be gone. In a second the VW would pick up speed as Mary completed the turn and headed toward the highway. Lisa took a deep breath and looked out the window. Outside—darkness. Black trees and shrubs moving toward them and away were slowing down, almost to a stop. Lisa knew there was grass beyond the asphalt before the fence. If she could jump free onto the grass, feet first. If . . .

She pressed down on the handle and pushed. The door flew

open and she launched herself, not feet first, as she'd hoped, but head first, her arms held out in front of her to break her fall. She hit hard, her outstretched palms smacked grass, her jeans ripped as her right hip scraped asphalt.

In the moment of impact she knew only that she'd done it. She was free. Of the car. Of Mary. Of the deadly knife. She tried to ignore the searing pain along her right side. Mary would speed off, try to save herself as best she could without her hostage.

But even as she began to sit up, testing for breakage, she sensed that Mary was not behaving as expected. She should be driving as fast as she could toward the highway, trying to make her getaway before Lieutenant Cohen and the others realized that her hostage had escaped. But the car was not speeding away down the road. For just a moment the car seemed to hang suspended, its lights picking up a fallen tree beside the road. Then it backed up quickly with a furious grinding of gears, its open door flapping.

Shocked, Lisa felt the headlights moving toward her, illuminating first the fence to her left and the grass in front of it, then moving steadily toward her as the car turned in her direction. Lisa gasped as she realized that Mary was hunting her in the darkness. And she was helpless, half-sitting in this open patch of grass, still dazed and weak from her head injury, her arms and her whole right side aching and bruised.

Her only hope was the fence. If she could get to it in time. She began to crawl toward it just at the moment that Mary's headlights reached her. Caught in the lights, she pulled herself along the grass toward the fence as fast as she could. Racing for her life, Lisa could hardly believe that Mary would do this—jeopardize her chance for escape in order to hurt her. Kill her. Why should Mary be trying to kill her instead of saving herself? Then Mary's words came back to her. "I will kill anyone who stands in the way of my freedom," she had said in that icy cold voice. I am doing that, Lisa realized. I am standing in the way of her freedom by depriving her of the hostage she needs to ensure her escape.

The VW was almost on her, coming fast. Lisa slid under the fence over slippery grass as hot metal grazed her arm. The fence shattered with a deafening sound. Above her, Lisa saw the VW sail through air in a shower of splintering fence rails, passenger door still flapping, wheels spinning.

The car crashed through bushes, landed on its side briefly, then rolled down the hill. It was shaken by an explosion and continued rolling until finally it settled uneasily at the bottom of the hill, its front end almost in the reservoir, its headlights still on, and flames licking out of its windows.

Footsteps pounded above Lisa's head. Blue-uniformed men burst through the broken fence, raced down the slope beside her. Lisa couldn't take her eyes off the burning car, at rest now except for the open door that still seemed to quiver.

Strong arms lifted her.

Sam's voice: "Maybe I shouldn't move you."

The lifting stopped. He was kneeling before her. "Lisa."

"Dove?" Lisa asked. "She okay?"

"She's okay."

"And Jean? The nurse?"

"Just a mild concussion."

"She was trying to kill me," Lisa whispered. "Instead of getting away, she came back to, to . . ." She tried to get up. Sam helped her.

From below, a shout. "She's dead. Get the lieutenant."

Lisa put her face in her hands. Then she looked at Sam. "I know she tried to kill us because we knew too much. But this time . . . I thought she'd just keep going, but she backed up and tried to run me down. That's how it happened, how she went through the fence."

"I know. I saw."

Lisa looked at his face, swimming in and out of focus. "Why did she have to do that?"

Sam said, "Forget her. You never knew her—you knew a madwoman obsessed with her brother's death."

Lisa nodded, but she couldn't stop thinking about the Mary she had known and cared about. She fought back the sob rising in her throat. Sam was right. The Mary she thought she knew had never existed. Mary's smile. Her humor. Her warmth.

Later, after she and Sam had been treated at the hospital and had talked to Lieutenant Cohen, Sam drove Lisa back to Dove's house to pick up her car. Then, over Sam's protests, Lisa drove back to Cambridge alone. The events of the evening kept rising up in her mind like images from a nightmare.

Thinking about Sam calmed her. They would be good friends. Only that. But it was comforting to know. Was it only last night that she and Brad had made love? She remembered her powerful desire for him. Over. Now, at last, she knew she could forget him. Funny. The advice Mary had given her had worked in a way. She had followed her heart straight to the bedroom with Brad—one last time. She had let him prove to her again what she already knew—that although he was attractive to her, he was not capable of the kind of love she required. As she pulled into the parking lot of her apartment building, she felt sad, but somehow strengthened. She couldn't wait to take a hot shower and get into bed.